JUST BETWEN FRIENDS

by Frank Sol

Copyright 2015 Cosmic Legends Publishing

Drafts2Digitial Edition, License Notes

Hotty Scotty

We all staggered into the apartment sometime after one, still giggling from the joking around in the back of the taxi. We'd had enough to drink during our night out that we currently weren't feeling any pain. The bar had been packed with hot college-aged guys and beautiful girls and we'd partied harder than Fred and I were used too doing. We were much into bars, but Scotty had invited us out with his buddies and we had accepted.

Given that the master bedroom was the largest room in the apartment, we all ended up stumbling in there.

Scotty fired up the computer.

I sprawled out on the queen-sized bed and stared up at the ceiling.

Fred brought a couple of *Smirnov Ices* from the fridge. I slugged a good dose of mine back in one long swallow.

Scotty was really cute. Baby-faced. Green eyes. Blond hair. He was young, he was hot, and he knew it.

But did he know that Fred and I both wanted him?

He wanted to stay overnight with us, in the spare bedroom, so that he would not to have drive back into town early for work after celebrating his new job with his other friends at one of the local bars. That made perfect sense of course, him not wanting an hour's drive home after partying and then having to get up and come back into town a few hours later for work. We'd said *yes* in an instant to his request; the chance to ogle him for the night was just too good to pass up.

Maybe we can get him drunk and willing to have a little man-to-man fun, Fred had commented to me when he'd told me that Scotty had first suggested crashing here for the night.

I have no problem with that, I'd replied with a grin.

Now here we all were.

"Now she's hot." Scotty was logged into some chat room, flirting outrageously with some woman in the States.

"Hundreds of kilometers away," I muttered. "A complete waste of time for everyone involved." I'd taken my t-shirt and pants off and was lounging on the bed in just my purple silk boxers. Officially I was reading a novel, but in actuality I was enjoying my view of Scotty. Blond hair, strong chin, pretty green eyes. A total stud.

Fred was perusing one of his car magazines and idly stroking my leg with his hand.

"Have I shown you guys my new tat?" Scotty asked suddenly.

"No."

I nodded. "You're holding out on us, Scotty."

"I didn't know you had any *old* tats," Fred added.

Scotty stood up and pulled his t-shirt over his head. Okay, he *peeled* off his snug gray t-shirt, revealing his well-defined chest. He was hairless—natural not shaved—and his biceps rippled nicely. Not overly muscled, but nice. Very nice. The waistband of his boxers was showing above his *Tommy* jeans.

The tat was of the Superman emblem.

"So you're Scotty Superman?" I teased.

"Yep," he replied with another of his boyish grins.

"The man of *steel*?" I asked, licking my lips.

"Yep."

"I'd like to see that," I muttered.

"Maybe I'll show it later."

"Promises, promises."

"You are so wasted." Fred giggled as he watched Scotty down most of a second *Smirnov* in one long swallow.

"But I'm friggin' happy," Scotty told us.

We just shook our heads.

"Ah, the energy of youth," I murmured. "And the stamina I hope."

Scotty turned back to his chatting.

I leaned towards Fred and kissed him. "You're wonderful," I told him in a soft voice.

"So are you," he replied.

I dropped my hands down to the fly of his blue *Wrangler* jeans. "You're getting hard," I told him in a low tone. I glanced over at Scotty. "No surprise why though." I was already semi-hard in my own boxers and had been for most of the night. One reason I'd been lying on my stomach.

He looked surprised by my openness. "What are you trying to do?"

"Have some fun."

"What about him?"

"*What* about him?" I repeated with a shrug. "Maybe he'll get a bit interested, or so we can hope." I pulled his t-shirt up to expose his almost-hairless chest and began nibbling at his left nipple. He moaned and half-heartedly tried to push me away. I just chuckled at his feeble attempts and pushed him onto his back.

In a moment, we were seriously kissing and making out. I pulled off his t-shirt and was nibbling at his tender nipples. Fred loved it when I did that. He and I both had a weakness for nipple play...tweaking them tended to set us both off. I often referred to them his 'on switches'.

Scotty seemed to be totally oblivious to us making out behind him.

Fred was naked and I was enjoying the sight. He had the kind of body-type that I liked. Average, not skinny but not muscular either. A thin patch of hair between his pecks. Not much body hair anywhere else either, but it was what I liked to see on a guy. I was hairy, but Fred liked hairy guys...so I was lucky that way. My boxer shorts were long gone as well and I was on top of him. We were kissing and running our hands all over each other's bodies. We weren't being quiet or shy about it either.

Abruptly, Scotty got up from the computer and left the room.

"Pity," Fred muttered.

"Damn." Scotty was hot...I wanted to see *him* naked.

Scotty walked back into the bedroom. He wasn't wearing his blue jeans now; just some stripped cotton boxer shorts.

"Wow," I said.

"I'm just getting ready to join you," he said nonchalantly. He hurried back into the hallway and we heard water running in the bathroom.

Fred was stroking my cock with his hand. "Did he just say what I thought I heard him say?"

I was idly rubbing his nipples. "I damn well hope so."

Scotty returned to the bedroom, naked.

"You're uncut!" I said.

"Yep." Surprisingly, he was totally comfortable with being naked in front of two horny gay men.

"You never told me that," I accused.

Fred shrugged. "I haven't seen him naked before," he replied. Scotty had been his friend for years before Fred had met me. "He's never taken off more than just his shirt before though." He was openly eying his friend, studying every inch of skin. "I've been missing out on a lot apparently."

"I hope you like kissing." I leaned towards Scotty who laughed a bit nervously.

He didn't back away though.

He had a pierced tongue—we could see the piercing when he talked. I'd never kissed anyone with a pierced tongue before so I was looking forward to the experience.

The piercing felt a bit strange as my tongue examined it.

Scotty kissed back with passion, though with some clumsiness.

I moved slightly so I could nibble at his ear. "Gently," I whispered. "Take is slow and gentle."

Fred was nibbling Scotty's left nipple and the boy was moaning loudly. His hand gripped my erection and pulled at it.

I dropped down to suck at his cock and he moaned and writhed on the bed. "Oh yeah, oh yeah!" he gasped. "Suck it," he pleaded. "Oh baby yes!"

Fred was kissing him while I sucked on his manhood. "It keeps clicking against my teeth," he announced.

I kept sucking and my fingers stroked his smooth balls.

"You're a great kisser!" he told me.

"You're not half-bad yourself."

"Had a lot of practice," he replied with false modesty.

"I bet you have." I kissed him again, feeling his hard cock pushing against my thigh.

"Fuck, I'm getting close."

"Good." I was leaking pre-cum big-time and I knew I wouldn't last very much longer.

Fred was stroking himself for all he was worth. I reached up to tweak his right nipple and Scotty pawed at his left. Fred's eyes rolled back in his head and he came with a loud grunt.

The hot cum splattering against his chest was too much for Scotty to take. He dropped his own hand down to his cock and gave it a few quick strokes. "Oh fucking God!" He shot out thick ropey strands of cum. He kept grunting as he came.

I scooped up some of that goo and used it as lube on myself. I loved doing that with Fred's cum and Scotty's was just as good. "Oh yeah!" I shot all over my own stomach.

We lay there for the rest of the night, limbs entwined, exhausted, drunk, but happy.

Confessions

"I've got something to tell you."

"What?" I asked as I closed the kitchen door behind us.

Fred sighed.

"What?"

"Last night something happened."

"A lot happened last night." I shook my head as I tried to think back on the events of the night before. "From what I can recall, we drank a lot of shooters, ate some chips, played cards, and passed out." I laughed. "I recall the cards and the shooters...but I don't recall going up to the bedroom." It was a really good thing that our friend Suzanne had a large house with some spare bedrooms. "We'd never have made it home on our bikes last night."

"You don't recall anything?"

"Not after the drinks. I slept pretty soundly until waking up next to you this morning." I was feeling somewhat horny at that point...sex in a friend's house could be fun, but not with a cat and four dogs watching your every move. *No privacy at all.*

"After you and Sue staggered upstairs, I walked Dan home." He lived just up the street from his sister. "Sue wanted to show you some new blouse or something. You never came back downstairs."

"I seem to vaguely recall something about wearing a tea cozie on our heads."

"Yes, you did."

"Damn, I was hoping that memory was just a dream."

"Well, you never came back down and Leanne had vanished somewhere earlier that night as well."

"She threw up in the chip bowl, didn't she?"

"I walked Dan home."

"You made it the whole four houses then?"

"Yep. Leanne wasn't there either. So we headed upstairs."

"Oh?"

"He wanted to show me some clothes he was getting rid of."

"Anything good?"

"Some t-shirts I liked. The jeans were too tight though."

"Dan does favor snug clothes." He did indeed. Maybe too tight for his own good...he usually dressed like he was trying to prove something. *He's a thirty-something trying to dress and act eighteen.* "He has the body for them though."

"So I was trying a shirt on. Dan had his own tee off by that point too, claimed he was too hot up there. He has a really nice hairy chest."

"Yes, he does." We had seen Dan shirtless on more than one occasion. It was always a nice sight and one we plotted to try and arrange more often. "That is your weakness."

"Well, one thing led to another."

"With Dan it usually does. He's a big flirt, always having ready with some sexual innuendo to liven things up."

"He made some comment about his jeans being too tight. So I reached over to check. He had a serious bulge in there. It was so frigging obvious. So...I took a chance and reached over to start stroking it and...."

"And?"

"He didn't object."

"Really?" My eyes widened.

"No, he just looked at me. That was encouragement enough that I took a chance and kissed him. He's a good kisser. Fuck, he's a *great* kisser. I love the feel of his beard against my check. Just like I like the feel of yours," he added hastily.

I smiled. "Good save."

Fred smiled back.

"So then what happened?"

"He unzipped his jeans and pulled them off, yanked off his briefs as well. I dropped my jeans and we got on the bed."

"In a married man's bed?" I gasped with mock horror. "Have you no shame at all?"

"None. We were kissing and I was sucking him off. He was moaning and really getting into it."

"And then?"

"Then we heard Leanne downstairs calling to us."

"Ouch." I winced.

"We scrambled for our clothes. Well, our jeans anyway. Dan went to the top of the stairs to slow her down. Told her that we were just trying on some of his old clothes that he was getting rid of."

"The truth...in a way."

"She was so out of it at that point, I don't think she would've noticed anything amiss."

"Or so you hope."

"I'm sorry."

"It's okay." I hugged him. "Just try to include me next time."

"I'll do my best."

"You are terrible," I told him. "One cheating incident and you break down and confess everything less than twelve hours later."

"Yep." Fred hung his head sheepishly.

"I like you that way." I kissed him again.

After we had taken our tea out to the living room, I decided to tell Fred about an experience of my own. We were both settled on the couch, me leaning up against his side with his arm around me.

"Back in the spring, Dan asked me to help him do some painting."

"On his house?"

"Yeah. Not his whole house, just in his kitchen and dining room. He called me and asked if I could help, and I told him I'd never painted anything before. So I might just be the world's worst painter, but he told me to come over anyway.

"You were working one of your forty hour weeks, so you had already gone to work. We were in our slow season and had lots of time off."

"I hate those three-day weeks you get."

"I know."

"So you went painting?"

"Yep, I went."

"I vaguely recall you mentioning that you went over to help him paint. You never said much about it though."

I shrugged. "What is there to say?"

"A lot apparently...or so I would now guess." He sipped his tea. "You were telling me that you went over to help him paint?" he prompted.

"We started with the ceiling, and because we were both so bad at it, we both ended up with paint splattered all over us." I smiled at the memory. Dan is drop-dead gorgeous: a slender runner's build, beautiful blue eyes, short brown hair and goatee, and is thirty but looks barely mid-twenties. "He was wearing tight cut-off blue jeans and a navy blue t-shirt; I was in *Levis* and a blue-green striped t-shirt.

"We got the ceiling done, but our heads and chests were covered in white paint, and my jeans were also pretty splashed. Dan wanted to stop and 'clean up', but I thought we should at least finish the walls, which we did with a bit more mess. Thank God for drop cloths!

"Anyway, he looked so cute with white paint splashed over his body. I'd spent most of the day with a major hard-on in my jeans."

"I'll bet you did." Fred sipped at his tea.

"He then said we should take showers—his house has only the one bathroom you know—but I had other ideas. I suggested that we should get the paint off our clothes before it dried, and he agreed. So we both went outside, uncoiled his garden hose, and proceeded to scrub each other's clothes. At least, that's how it started.

"The t-shirts came off so we could get the paint off our chests, and by then his shorts and my jeans were soaking and sagging, revealing more white paint on his navy blue *Hanes* briefs and my black *Calvin* boxers.

"So first we got all the paint off our pants, and then they came off, and we went to work on each other's undies. For him, it was all just a simple friendly clean up. For me, it was a dream come true. Dan in wet clinging briefs? Woo hoo." I was getting hard just thinking about it! Talk about *wet dreams*! "And he still thinks I did him a favor!"

Fred laughed. "That sounds like Dan. So what happened next?"

"I put my wet clothes back on and biked home." I shrugged. "A let down, I know."

"Yeah. I wish we had gotten farther with him. Damn wife."

"So we've both had some fun with him...but not as much as we would like."

"No, not quite as much as we would like."

We shared a devious smile. "We'll have to see about changing that."

"You know, I had a fantasy..."

"No kidding?" The sarcasm was heavy in my voice. Fred had been in lust with Dan, ever since first laying eyes on him. Somewhat to Fred's surprise and delight, they had become friends, through me; Dan knew that we both were gay and figured it was okay since we had been friends for so long and, up until last night, had never "hit on him". We spent a lot of time doing "guy" things, so Dan figured we were just a gay couple who were a "*friends*".

"He never anticipated what would happen that Saturday when he asked me to trim his hair for him," Fred told me.

Dan arrives at our house in shorts and a t-shirt, his muscular, taut body accentuated by his snug-fitting athletic apparel. I was instantly aroused, as I usually am when Dan was around. It was a battle hiding the bulge in my pants

most of the time, but I had managed to do it many times. I had been planning this day for weeks. He had to have Dan! He ached for him! He just hoped he could keep the situation under control and not scare Dan away forever.

"Hey, Dan," Fred greeted his friend at the door, "come on in."

"How ya doin'?" Dan asked his friend.

"Okay. Let's go into the kitchen and get this haircut over with, shall we?" I lead Dan into the kitchen where I had placed a chair in the middle of

the room so I could walk around him as I trim his hair. "I'll get a towel to catch the hair as I cut it, okay?"

"Sure, whatever," Dan answered, noticing how neatly Fred had set up the table with scissors, brush, comb, etc.

I come back to the kitchen with a towel and Dan sits in the chair. I was anxiously anticipating having my hands on his body in *any* capacity.

I pick up the comb and part Dan's dampened hair into sections. I start with the top of his head first, lifting the hair with the comb and snipping it carefully. As I stand in front of Dan, our legs keep rubbing against each other and I find it impossible not to become aroused. I move my thighs against Dan's muscular legs as often as possible to feel his hot flesh against my own.

I move around to the back of Dan's hair and lean against him as I cut his hair, trying to get it straight all over Dan's head. I could feel my penis brush against him and the touch of his member on his back was torturous. I try not to lean into it and Dan keeps pushing forward.

"Shit! This is uneven. I'll have to trim it more on top."

I am in heaven. I look down and take note of Dan's penis. It seems to be semi-aroused. I decided to be a bit bolder. I slide my hands up Dan's shorts and began to fondle his testicles.

Dan doesn't move! He sits there and lets me play with his genitals. I move hand further up his thigh and discover that Dan has a raging erection!

"Dan, I want you," I say. "I've wanted you for a long time."

Dan inhales deeply and looks at his friend seriously. "I know, Fred."

"You do?"

"Yes. You are my best friend and if it will make you happy, I'll play along with you. I know it won't go any further, but I know you and I know that you'll never be able to live with yourself until your curiosity is satisfied."

"I just want to make love with you. I can't help it!"

Dan takes my head into his hands and bends over and kisses me on the lips, gently at first and then parting my lips with his tongue, he probes my mouth with his tongue, sucking and licking the sweet taste of me.

I continue to stroke and fondle Dan. Dan slides his shorts down and I moved to take Dan's penis into my mouth. Dan gasps and holds onto me as I suck him hungrily, milking his cock as I fondle his balls. Dan begins to slide his cock in and out of my mouth, pumping his member further and further down my throat until I can't take any more of it.

I suck hard and fast, seemingly starved for the milk hiding within his friend's erection. I pull the cock from my mouth. "Will you fuck me, Dan? Please? I have a condom here. I need to feel you inside me," Fred pleaded.

"I've never done it before. I don't want to hurt you."

"Don't worry, you won't."

"Okay then," Dan answers. He slides the condom over his erection and I pull down his shorts, revealing his tight buttocks. Dan lubricated my hole and proceeds to insert his penis a little bit at a time.

I'd waited this moment for so long! I am so eager to receive my new lover's cock into my body. Dan bends over and wraps his arms around me, taking my cock into one hand and my testicles into the other. He strokes and fondles me as he begins to slide in and out, slowly at first, until he had his erection fully inside me, excited by the tight, hot crevice wrapped around his love tool. "Faster," I say, backing my ass onto his friend's hard-on.

Dan begins to fuck me faster, struggling to refrain from releasing his cum too soon. He concentrates on bringing pleasure to me, instead of pleasing himself.

I am going insane with ecstasy! I struggle to keep this moment from ever ending!

We pause to rest and start again several times until the onslaught of climax cannot be unrestrained and we both cum with mighty shouts.

Bad Deeds Coming Home

"Dan's coming over," Fred told me as he put the phone back onto its little stand.

"Oh?" I raised an eyebrow.

"Yeah, he has those clothes for me."

"Kay." I went back to perusing my emails on the computer. "Is that his story?"

There was a knock at the door.

I opened it. "Hi, Dan. Come on in."

He was looking a little awkward as he stood in the doorway. "Hey, Mike. I brought those shirts over for Fred to have."

Fred took the bag from him. "Thanks. I forgot to swing by and get them yesterday morning."

"Hard to manage carrying a bag like that home on a bike," I added. "So what's new?"

Dan shrugged. "We're still recovering from the other night."

"How's Leanne?"

"Cranky, so I think she's back to normal."

We laughed at that.

"I was thinking about dying my hair," he told us. "For the department charity fund. If they raise a certain amount, say a hundred bucks, then I'll dye my hair some outrageous color."

"How about a *crimson* red?" I asked pointedly. "Maybe shave the sides into a letter A? You know, a scarlet letter."

Dan looked at me. "He knows?" Dan asked.

"I told him everything when we got home," Fred admitted sheepishly.

"I know everything you shameless hussy!" I marched up to Dan and waved my fist in his face. "He confessed everything the second we got home!" I hadn't realized how tall Dan was until I got so close to him. "Taking drunken advantage of my boyfriend." I put a lot of menace into my voice. "You have some nerve buddy!"

"Hey," Dan protested, raising his hands in defense and looking worried, "it was just one of those things. I never meant any harm."

"No harm?"

"No. Look, I'm sorry."

"How sorry?" I asked.

"Really sorry." He looked so upset, so lost.

"I'm sorry too," I told him.

Dan looked puzzled.

"I'm sorry I missed seeing it." I grabbed Dan's crotch and gave it a little squeeze. "I hear that it was quite a sight." He felt flaccid in my hand, but the bulge in those jeans was nothing to belittle either.

He looked startled by the sudden change in my tone and demeanor.

I stretched up my neck and kissed him.

He was obviously startled, but he recovered quickly and kissed me back and then we were locking lips. The feel of his well-trimmed goatee against my face was nice—Fred was clean-shaven and couldn't grow a decent beard to save his life.

Fred was standing there watching us.

"Let's see what you've got." I pulled Dan's gray t-shirt up and over his head. I had seen him *sans* shirt numerous times at both his house and at our apartment during the hot summer months. He relied on Fred for haircuts after all. His chest was nicely furry and well defined. He had a bit of a belly, but was pretty much an average thirty-something guy.

I tossed my t-shirt onto the floor. It landed on top of Dan's. Fred was still stripping, but he was also kissing Dan without stop. The two of them were getting seriously into it.

I found the sight very arousing.

Dan was stripped down to his navy blue briefs. "They're not the best," he apologized as he dropped his blue jeans onto the pile of discarded clothing.

"They look fine."

Fred shook his head. "They look better on the floor." He pulled them down to suit his words.

Dan's cock bobbed up and I got my first look at it.

I was not disappointed—he was fairly well hung, just as he so had often advertised. "You have a great body," I told him. Athletic but not overly so. I was so totally not into muscle-jocks or gym bunny types. He had a slightly above-average body. He was hot.

"I need to get running again. I'm getting a tummy."

"It looks fine," I told him and I rubbed it. I had seen Dan's legs in shorts before, to say nothing of those wet briefs, but never had I seen him completely naked.

I was sorry it had taken this long to do so, but the wait had been worth it.

"Well, how about you?" Dan reached over and pulled my nylon shorts down with one swift yank. "Wow," he said.

"Wow?" I repeated. "I hear that a lot when I take my clothes off."

"I never thought a little guy like you would have such a big one." Dan was staring. He did look impressed.

"That's what I thought when I first saw him naked." Fred shook his head. "I was like 'you expect me to do *what* with that?'"

"You figured it out though, Fred."

"Yeah."

I stepped closer to Dan and he wrapped his warm fingers around my growing erection. "You have nice hands."

"Thanks." He sounded shy.

I pushed Dan back onto the couch. I went down on him, taking his hard cock into my mouth and teasing it with my tongue.

Dan moaned as I sucked on him.

Fred was kissing him full on the lips.

I had Fred's hand on my cock and Dan's hand playing with my balls. The mingling sensations were incredible. Sex with Fred was all well and good, but there was something to be said for a third set of hands.

We shifted positions, and I was sucking at Fred's cock while Fred and Dan were kissing. Dan was stroking himself. *So many limbs*, I thought.

Dan grunted loudly as he came. Hell, he *shouted* as he came. He was very noisy. He shot a lot and it splattered across my chest.

I smeared the white goo down to my cock and stroked myself more quickly. Using the cum from another man was another of my turn-ons...not sure just what I found so arousing about it, but it really got me worked up.

Fred leaned in close and we kissed each other, probing our tongues deeper and deeper. Fred grunted and he and I came at the same time.

Dan collapsed limply onto the couch. I slumped onto the floor.

Fred and I looked at each other.

"Sounded like it was a good one."

"Oh it was," he gasped. "That was amazing."

"No hard feelings then."

"No, nothing hard now." Dan looked at his now-flaccid cock. "You were fucking amazing," he told me.

I wiped sweat from my brow. "I do my best."

Dan stood up and picked up his briefs. "I guess I should get going." Then he started pulling on his jeans over his long legs.

Fred nodded. "Yeah, Leanne will be waiting."

"Yep." Dan left his t-shirt untucked. "Wow, guys." He sounded awkward. "That was pretty hot."

"Yes. You were great."

"Yep. No hard feelings about anything. I'm glad you stopped by."

"So am I." Dan snatched his keys from the counter. "See ya at work."

"Bye, Dan!"

"To think," I commented after Dan had left for home, "all those times at the apartment when he was over. We could have had him then."

"What were we thinking?"

"Well, we know now." I smiled and leaned back on the couch. "I look forward to the next time."

Strip Poker

Dan, being the host that evening, was the natural leader. He suggested that we play poker. A small argument ensued about money and our general lack of it at the time, and it was Dan who finally suggested that we play strip poker instead. At first, there was silence. After about ten seconds that seemed like hours, Fred nodded. "Sure, why the hell not?"

I could scarcely conceal my excitement. This was gonna be good.

Fred got out the cards and we sat on the couch and chairs around a coffee table. Fred and Dan set out the very simple rules. We'd play five cards, two draws, the worst hand lost one item of clothing. Watches and rings did not count; shoes and socks were considered as pairs to be "one item".

"Sounds fair enough to me," I commented. "Deal 'em out."

The first few hands went quickly and nervously. There was a lot of smirking and bluffing that's for sure. After all of us had lost our shoes and socks, and I was losing (winning?) with my t-shirt gone as well. The next few hands went rather well for me, and pretty soon all three of us were shirtless.

The next hand was pretty tense, that was for sure. We were all down to just our jeans and underwear. You'd have thought we were playing for million dollar stakes if you just went by the tension in the air. It was very exciting and I knew then that something was going to happen. You could just feel it in the air. We were all very horny and more than half-drunk, and feeling the general atmosphere, I really and truly hoped we would get into some good old boyish "horsing" around.

Anyway, I lost that hand, and to much jeering, I stood up and took off my jeans. I didn't hesitate. It actually felt kind of cool stepping out of my jeans and standing in the middle of somebody else's living room in just my red briefs and being looked over by my two good looking friends. My dick was half-hard already, and their staring certainly didn't help. I was having fun, and I didn't care if I lost.

The next hand was slow, as the high-tension game got even tenser. Fred lost the next hand and took off his blue work pants to reveal a pair of standard white briefs. No doubt about it, Fred had a hard-on, pointing straight up and making a perfect "tent". Dan and I ribbed him about his "little boner", while my own hastily growing erection was constrained by pointing straight downwards and having nowhere to grow to. It was at precisely that moment, Fred pointed to my own crotch and announced, "Now that's a boner!"

After the laughter and the jeers settled down again, I dealt out the next hand of cards.

This time Dan lost his jeans and exposed a fantastic pair of sky-blue bikini-style briefs and a raging erection that pointed towards his hip. The tiny

fabric of his underwear barely constrained Dan's obviously good-sized dick.

That left the three of us in our underwear. All three of us were rock hard and leaking small wet spots into our underwear. The next hand was crucial and intense.

Fred's "jack-high" looked pretty lame until Dan showed us his "ten-high, almost flush". With incredible excitement, I watched as Dan boldly got up and stripped off his sexy bikini briefs and stood there naked as a jaybird and his big thick cock pointing straight out at me. It was big all right, and he even had a patch of light brown pubes tonight. By this time, my erection was straining the fabric of my cotton briefs.

It was then that Dan announced that we had to play until there was a winner. The winner is the only one who has some clothes on when everyone else is naked. This allowed the game to go on, but Fred was unsure of Dan's status since he had no more clothes to lose, and I was curious about what the winner would win.

Dan, being his usual and arrogant self, answered first, that he could play on and lose only one more time. The next time he lost, or anyone else in his predicament, then they would be the "ultimate loser" and have to jerk off the "ultimate winner".

We all looked at each other, thinking over this new twist. I of course

thought it an excellent idea. Sure enough, Fred agreed, stating, "Why the fuck not?"

I said "Ok" and Dan nodded.

The last few hands were wildly exciting. We both wanted to win now.

Dan, of course, was out of it. We figured Dan that would be the one to "ultimately lose", so we felt better about our chances. I found it really hard to concentrate on the cards with Dan sitting there naked with his thick boner sticking up!

I wanted to win and have Fred lose. I really wanted to watch him have to jerk Dan off. That would be so hot.

Instead, I lost the next hand and exposed my erection for my friends to see. It was still a hoot.

With two of us naked, that made Fred the "ultimate winner". To decide the "ultimate loser", the pair of us naked losers had to play one last hand. The stakes were very high indeed as the loser had to jerk off Fred!

I debated throwing back my two Kings, but decided I would rather take my chances because I considered both guys to be hot and sexy.

As it turned out, Dan lost the last hand and to much jeering and joking, got on his knees in front of Fred and proceeded to give him a hand job. I watched intently as Dan began to stroke Fred's cock. He just gripped the shaft and slid his hand back and forth, sliding the skin back and forth over Dan's mushroom shaped head.

Fred gave Dan some encouragement and further instructions. Dan began to move his hands faster and Fred started to moan with pleasure.

I began to stroke myself quickly. I just couldn't help it any longer. It was so hot watching my partner having his cock stroked by another guy. Call me nuts, but I liked what I saw. I moved closer and started to stroke Dan's cock. He seemed startled at first, but he certainly made no objections to my presence or touching him.

Fred didn't seem to notice us and just laid back on his chair and moaned. It didn't take long for either of us to catch up with him. After a minute or two of this double jerk-off session, Fred announced that he was going to cum and immediately shot a healthy load of white gobs onto his chest.

With that, I started to cum, almost at the same time. My load landed on the carpet in front of me. Dan grunted and his dick twitched. Cum splattered along Fred's leg.

"Wow," I said.

Fred shook his head. "That was fun."

Dan was panting. "I got so horny. I couldn't help myself."

"No crime in that."

"Yep." I looked around. "We should get cleaned up." I smiled. "Although, we do have most of the night still free."

"I don't have the energy left for another game," Fred complained.

"You can watch then." I reached over to stroke my fingers along Dan's hairy chest yet again. "We can have some more fun here. We're all just friends right?"

Drawn

I was so busted!

Here I was, kneeling between Dan's knees, his half-hard cock, still oozing cum pressed against my t-shirt. His cum was beginning to liquefy and soak into the fabric, and I had no idea just how long Fred had been sitting there, sketching us! My redhead's skin betrayed me again as I turned the color of tomato juice. I was beginning to feel like my skin had never been any other color than red. "Fred, I...I mean I didn't...." didn't what? Didn't mean to jack Dan off? There was still cum dripping from my fingers.

Dan nodded. "I...I'm sorry, too."

"Dan," Fred said with a smile in his voice. "Dan, it's alright."

Dan shrugged somewhat guiltily.

"I knew Fred wouldn't mind." I ran my fingers along Dan's chest and watched him tremble. "Anyway, it's just Dan."

"Oh thanks," he said.

"He means it, Dan." I smiled. "Fred is right. It's just Dan."

Dan shook his head.

I pulled him closer to me again and kissed him again, my tongue exploring his mouth. I froze for a second, and then melted into his embrace. As our tongues dueled in my mouth, I realized I was missing the taste of his cum.

After what seemed to be a minute or two, but I guess was quite a bit longer, Fred interrupted us.

"Dan, your shirt's a mess. Give it to me and I'll wash it. I don't want you going home with cum stains all over your shirt."

"No one will be home yet, but thanks, I'd rather not take the chance."

I broke my clinch with Dan and he quickly peeled off his Leafs t-shirt. As he handed it to Fred, he smiled.

"I was hoping to see you get that shirt off. You've got a better chest than I could ever hope for. Nice pecs." He ran a finger, appreciatively over my upper chest and across a nipple. "You've got an awesome build."

Dan gave a laugh. He could be surprisingly quiet-mouthed about how hot he looked.

Fred wanted us to go out to the backyard and sit for a while more, but Dan said he had to leave. We stood there talking a while until Dan finally picked up his discarded jeans from the floor, and then he stopped and looked at me.

"Mike, believe me, I don't think you're fat." He put those big hands of his under my arms, it felt like they went totally around my chest, and lifted me off my feet until my head was finally level with his. He kissed me hard, his lips mashing mine against my teeth. My hands went around his neck and my legs wrapped around his hips without my thinking about it. As he forced his tongue deeper into my mouth, I rubbed my nylon shorts encased dick against his stomach as I felt his dick rise up and press against the seat of my pants, hard and insistent. I was pulling his head against my face as I devoured his tongue. His lightly haired chest felt great against my hairy one.

"Okay, okay," Fred laughed. "Dan, I'll make sure Mike returns your shirt later. Now either get dressed and get out of here or get Mike undressed and finish what you've started!"

That kind of pulled me up short and I backed off. Dan just laughed and

finally set me down on my feet again.

"I'll see you guys later," Dan said. Then he turned away and started putting on his clothes.

"Here, Mike, look at these while I see Dan out."

Fred handed me his pad. I sat down on the edge of the bed and started looking through the used pages. They were all pretty rough sketches, just good approximations of the positions so they could be fleshed out later. If you didn't know it was me, it could have been anyone. In one, I was kneeling between Dan's thighs, my hand holding his hard dick pressed against my cheek. In another, I was looking; it almost looked like in awe, at his dick as I stroked it. The final one in the series was a sort of a close up (from an angle Fred really couldn't have seen) of Dan's dick spurting and cum running over my hand with a face in the background. The eyes were wide, mesmerized by what the hand was doing.

I was barely aware as Dan and Fred left the room. These rough sketches were dominating my attenion. I continued to flip through the pad. There was another young guy, longish hair, really well built, climbing up a tree that I recognized from the neighborhood park. It looked like most of the time his dick was half-hard, arching away from his body.

Fred came back and sat down next to me on the couch. He put his arm over my bare shoulders and looked at the sketchpad. "These are all just rough sketches, you know, quick figure placement and all. Would you like to see my finished work?"

"Yes, that would be great!"

He walked over to his desk and brought out three portfolio books, each about sixteen by twenty. He opened the first one and laid it across both our laps and his arm returned to rest across my shoulders. "These are some of my favorite models."

The sketches were all finished work, most of them pen and ink on what looked to be expensive parchment paper; they were all signed and dated.

But the naked men! Thin men, muscular men, gym builds, work builds, they were sitting or lying down, climbing trees or swimming. All of them were smiling and happy, really enjoying what they were doing. All of them looked to be slightly aroused, but they didn't have erections. They weren't all well- endowed either. They looked like the same cross-section of sizes I saw at the gym or changing room at the pool. They were just happy, well-built men enjoying being naked.

"When did you do these?"

"Over the years."

"And you've been holding out on me all this time?"

"Well..." he shrugged. "There aren't really all that great. I just dabbled a bit."

"You have great talent, Fred." I turned back to the pages. I'd never really had as many chances to look at naked guys before. I mean, I checked guys out in the locker room and all, like everyone else and occasionally looked for a second or two at an exceptionally well-built guy at the pool, but I never really had the chance to look before. Well, not since before getting the 'Net anyway. But these drawings! These guys were awesome! The way their muscles moved, the tension, the way their dicks swung, it totally absorbed me. I began to see how great they looked, how hot they were.

Fred was sitting closer to me now, his hand cupping my shoulder opposite him. We were approaching the halfway point in the book, when I saw him. "That's Dan!"

"Yep."

"God, he's hot." Then I blushed, I hadn't meant to say that aloud.

"He is all that," Fred laughed. "He's one of my fave subjects. You'll see him a lot in the next few books."

I turned the page: Dan sitting at a table eating. Dan running. Dan as an angel. Dan carrying boxes. Dan doing gymnastics, Dan, Dan, Dan, and all naked. I was loving it. Okay, I confess it. There were quite a few pictures of other guys too, I just wasn't looking at them very closely, I kept looking for Dan! Then the pictures started to change. The guys were in more erotic poses;

their dicks were a good bit bigger. I almost started flipping the pages looking for Dan.

Fred laughed. "Okay, okay! I'll get you Dan's book. I keep a special portfolio of each of my special models." As he walked away, he added: "I hope I'll have one of you soon."

Yeah, right, I thought. Fred would never get around to sketching me. He had other interests. Right? I glanced down at my shorts. They were straining with a serious bulge. Stroking Dan had gotten me so horny, and even if it hadn't happened, I guess I knew what was likely to happen here when I brought him upstairs to show him the new flooring in my office.

"Here you go, Mike, These are my favorites of Dan."

This time when he sat down, I leaned against him, feeling the texture of his shirt on my shoulder. He reached his arm over my shoulders again and this time, his hand reached down and rested on my biceps, I felt the fingers begin a little slow stroking motion.

Good, I thought, he's interested.

When he started to turn the pages of the book, though, I totally got involved with Dan again. After the first five or six poses, though, the sketches started to change. They seemed a lot more provocative. Dan sitting, on the couch, knee bent, looking straight out of the page, with a sexy half-smile and an obviously half-hard dick, Dan standing, running his hand down his lower stomach into his pubic bush, smiling out of the sheet. Several more erotic poses.

Finally, Dan standing in profile, foot up on a stool, elbow on his knee looking out and smiling, totally hard. It looked like he had a massive cock.

"How did you know he was that big?"

"I was guessing." Fred shrugged. "I took some of these at work...got my ideas seeing him sitting in the cafeteria or walking through the hallways. I never knew his name until you started working there."

"I thought he was hot the first time I saw him. Man, I had to keep reminding myself not to stand there and stare at him." I had been trying to keep a low profile at the time...no point in telling everyone I was gay when I was still just a temp in the place. Don't do anything to risk getting hired on later, Fred had told me.

"Me too. All the years I've been lusting after him, I never imagined we'd become friends or that we'd be more than just friends."

"How's that song lyric go? Friends with benefits?"

"Something like that." He skipped over several pages and stopped at some parts studies. Mid-thigh to shoulders were all that was included, that and Dan's enormous dick, hard and pressing up against his six pack. I snuggled up against Fred's chest.

"How does he stay hard long enough for you to sketch it?"

"I help him."

My eyes bulged. "He's modeled for you then?" I thought those were just from your imagination.

"Once or twice."

I could feel he was nuzzling my hair with his lips and nose, feel his warm breath on my scalp. "Would you help me?"

"Are you certain you want me to, Mike?"

"Yes."

His hand sort of drifted off my bicep and onto my chest, just his fingertips brushed over my peck and found my nipple where it stayed and teased for a bit. Then he leaned his face in and kissed me. My second guy-kiss of the afternoon! It was so different from Dan, not like he was hesitating or anything, but he just ran his tongue over my lips and waited till I let him in. I liked how it seemed that every guy kissed differently.

Fred was slow and gentle, but he felt like he was really strong at the same time, like he knew just what to do, so I just relaxed and let him. His hands, his fingers, really, wandered over my body, just lightly touching my stomach, my nipples, my thighs, then began to center around the drawstring of my shorts.

He eased his fingertips under my waistband, just ruffling the top of my pubic bush, then took them out and pulled my shorts down. I actually stopped breathing for a minute. He was going to do it! Fred was going to have sex with me. My dick was so hard; I could actually feel the pressure release as the zipper opened. Then it hit bottom.

Fred slid off the bed and spread my knees with his hands. He knelt between them and grabbed the top of my shorts, and slowly pulled them down off my legs, all the time looking at my crotch. I wasn't wearing underwear, so my dick sort of popped into the open as the shorts cleared it. Fred stopped, and I sort of heard a little catch in his breath.

Okay, I know I'm proud of my dick but Fred stared at it. Enjoy? Heck, he was in hypnotized by it! He was looking at it like it was some kind of work of art or something! No, not a work of art, something to eat. Something he really wanted to eat. "Suck me, Fred, please? Suck me."

He pulled my hips forward till my butt rested on the edge of the bed, and then he spread my legs and started licking my thighs, slowly, first one then the other, always getting closer to my balls. I was really trying to stay still and not move. I didn't want to do anything wrong, so I figured, I should just stay still and let him do it.

He put a hand under my balls, and lifted them, then touched them to his lips and kissed them, then started licking them, slowly, softly. Then he sucked one into his mouth and rolled it around on his tongue. Then the other, then both!

It was like electricity going through me! I could feel his tongue from my scalp to my toes! I grabbed the couch cushions and held on for dear life! The he started running his tongue up the shaft of my dick!

His tongue felt so warm and wet and I'd never felt anything like this before. It was so hard to just sit there! I wanted to move under his tongue. I was actually biting my lips and whimpering. I looked down and saw the top of his head and it's short dark hair. My dick was jutting above it, and I could see all the pre-cum dripping out from the tip.

Fred looked up at me, took my dick in his hand and smiled. I could see that his fingers just touched around the thickest part of the shaft, and he licked the pre-cum off the head! I threw my head back and started growling deep in my throat as I felt his skin the cover off the head of my dick.

I looked down to see the skin caught behind the head, just as he lowered his mouth onto my dick! God, it felt like it was sliding into fire! When he stopped, about half way down, I was so frustrated! I could feel the block in the back of his mouth, and realized I was at the opening of his throat. But I wanted my entire dick in his mouth; I wanted to really be in him! I started to push my hips up, then stopped. I couldn't do that! It wasn't right for me to force my dick into him like that! He was doing this for me; I couldn't try to get more than he offered! I might hurt him!

I heard a strange noise from Fred, like he was frustrated too? Like he wanted me to do something? What?! Fred pushed my hips back onto the bed so they hit the back. When I couldn't go any further back, I felt one of his hands take mine and put it on the back of his head, then the other hand. I was a little confused, until I felt him grab my hips and. As he slid his mouth down the shaft of my dick, he pulled my hips up to meet it. What? He pulled back, and I saw him look up at me, his lips white stretched around the shaft of my dick. He slid down again, and this time really pulled my hips up, I felt this almost 'pop' and my dick was clenched in the tightest, hottest place it had ever been!

Finally I got the idea; he wanted me to push into him! Once, till his nose was buried in my pubes, and out. Twice, pushing down on the back of his head. I started to pull back, but he followed me and all of a sudden, I felt this rhythmic clutching on my dick, like he was masturbating me with his throat!

That was it. I felt my dick swell in his throat, and felt him gag as it did. I erupted. I don't think I'd ever cum so hard!

"Wow, Mike!" Fred gasped. "That was amazing."

"You're telling me."

Fred stood up, and I could see the huge tent in his jeans and the wet spot in front. "Uh, Fred? Do you want me to do something for you? I mean, do you want me to do it to you now?"

"Only do what you really want to do. You don't have to do me just because I sucked you off."

"I want too."

Then he laughed. "Besides, I came when you did. First time in a long time I came without touching!"

I know it's silly, but that made me feel real proud, for some reason. Fred asked if I wanted a glass of wine, which I did, so he told me to go out to the patio and he'd meet me there. Then I realized I didn't know where my shorts got to, but what the heck? He'd just blown me; I didn't think he'd object if I went out naked, Dan had been out there naked earlier. A glass of wine sounded really good right now.

I was sitting down when he got there. "Good. I'm glad that you're comfortable enough to come out here naked. Now let's talk about you and Dan."

"He stopped by for a chat."

"And that involved you unzipping his jeans?"

"He had an itch."

"I see."

"So I was scratching it for him."

Fred laughed. "You're terrible, you know that?"

"Yeah...but you love me anyway."

Meeting With Jake

We had it all planned out.

We were friends after all. He and his partner had met up with Fred and I for coffee a couple of different times. Problem was, Fred and Rick didn't hit it off. But Jake and I had a few things in common, such as partners who worked longer hours than we did, as well as seriously overactive libidos.

Jake and I flirted outrageously on the 'net. We openly made sexual comments to each other. When we ran into each other in public, we flirted and made fleeting body contact.

So one day, while we were chatting on the 'net, I mentioned that I had the house to myself the next day.

Jake was intrigued and we made plans.

I would meet him at the park and then we would go to back to my house. I had been looking forward to this day all week. I couldn't wait to let my hands roam over his young, lean body. As I pulled into the parking lot of the park I immediately spotted him waiting by the planned meeting place.

I pulled up and he recognized me and gave me a warm smile. He was early and that was a good sign. It meant he was as eager as I was. I stopped my car and motioned for him to come over. He was wearing tight jeans that outlined his slim features and an unbuttoned polo shirt. I had to admit, that as usual, he looked very good. He always dressed expensively. He walked to the other side of my car and got in. He was still smiling. My eyes travelled up and down his body a couple of times. I liked what I saw. He had brown hair and beautiful dark brown eyes. This was one beautiful guy!

"Hi," I said as I offered my hand.

"Hi," he said as he returned my handshake.

The touch of his warm flesh brought my penis to life. I held his hand a little longer than would be normal as I looked into his eyes. His bold stare back right back at me told me he was ready for this meeting. I was equally ready to give him the pleasurable experience he desired.

As we drove away we made small talk about how warm it had gotten in recent days and talked about other stuff.

I stopped at the liquor store on the way and picked up some wine to help us relax back at the house. While there, I made certain to say hi to a friend who worked there. At times I was amazed at just how many gay guys I knew around town.

As Jake and I pulled into the driveway, my heart was pounding and again my penis began to rise. I pulled up close to the door and looked at him. I wanted to make sure he was ready for this. "We don't have to go in if you don't want to," I told him. "We could just forget the whole thing and go home. It's totally up to you," I reassured him.

"I want to," was his immediate answer. He gave me that stare again and I was happy to hear his answer.

I smiled at him and slowly laid my hand on his leg. I rubbed his thigh as we looked at each other. I took my hand away and opened the car door. We both got out and walked to the house. He walked slightly ahead of me and I had a good look at his nice ass. It was exactly as I had dreamed it would be. Nice and trim and I watched the sides pull in as he walked. By the time we got into the kitchen I had a full erection.

We went in and sat down in the living room—him on the edge of the couch and me in one of the chairs. We sipped our wine and starting talking. After the second glass, the conversation drifted to sex. He was telling me about the last time he had been fucked by Rick. "That was a couple of weeks ago," he told me. "He's been too tired the last few nights for any sex...and my hand just isn't the same as having another guy there doing it."

"Yeah," I replied. "Fred's been overworked lately too. We just cuddle up and sleep. Which is fine, but I need some action." By the growing bulges in our jeans, we were both aroused and excited.

I went over to the couch and sat next to him. I put my hand on his leg and rubbed it again. I looked at his crotch and saw the outline of his erection. I let me fingers gently brush across it. He was of a pretty good size and I couldn't wait to see it for real.

He was still sitting on the edge of the couch so I got on my knees between his legs. I reached up and started to slide my hands inside his unbuttoned shirt. "Oh yeah," he said as he leaned over to kiss me.

Jake lifted his shirt off, exposing his hairy chest and stomach. I let my hands run over his torso, feeling its firmness. I leaned forward and kissed his stomach. I then began to lick downward until I got to his navel. I let my tongue dart in and out of it. He started to breath hard and I was happy that I was able to turn him on. He put his hands on my head to push me lower but I wasn't ready yet.

"I want to give you a back rub first," I said. "Come upstairs." I led him up the stairs, my hand resting on the bulge in his jeans.

I pushed him onto the bed and told him to lay down on his stomach. He did so and buried his head in a pillow. I stood up and admired his body. His body was fairly hairy and I liked what I saw. Especially the perfectly shaped spheres of his ass that pointed up at me.

I started to rub him down and we both were really enjoying this. I was massaging him up and down his back. Every now and then I would lean over and let my tongue lick a small area and then massage it. I was getting so hot!

"How's it feel?" I asked him.

"Good," was all he said.

"Do you want your legs rubbed too?" I asked him.

He didn't even respond. He just reached down and undid the front of his Tommy jeans and started to slide them down his legs. I helped him get his tight jeans off as my eyes were glued to his butt. The only thing covering them now was the thin material of his Calvin Klein boxers.

I started at the bottom of one leg and rubbed up to his ass. He had a small amount of soft, dark hair on his legs. I then started on the other leg and worked my way up. When I got up to his ass again he started to tighten his ass up and push it into the bed. I put my hands on his ass and gently squeezed. He reared up and I let one hand slip under him and grab his penis. It was rock hard and he gave a loud sigh when I grabbed it.

Jake rolled over and pulled his underwear off. I was impressed with his penis. It was beautifully built with a nice head and I reached for it again. I started to stroke him. I leaned over brought my lips close to his balls. I let my tongue sample the soft objects. I started to lick his balls as I continued to stroke his cock. Then, I started to suck on his balls, rolling each one around my mouth with my tongue.

I slowly licked up to the top of his cock. He pushed his groin up and forced his cock into my mouth and I began to suck. I ran my tongue around the head of his cock while I sucked him off. My hands started to play with his balls. It didn't take him long. I felt his balls tighten and the head of his penis swell in my mouth. He started to pump his cock into my mouth and thrust his hips up. I fired his cum into my awaiting mouth and I swallowed all he had. I loved the taste of his young sperm.

I continued to suck until he had completed his intense orgasm. I let his penis fall from my mouth but it was still semi-erect. He laid breathing hard as I finally got around to removing my own shirt. I took his hand and placed it on my crotch. His hand squeezed what I had to offer and he smiled.

"Your turn," Jake told me. He began to undo my pants. I took them down for him and removed my Hanes underwear. He sat up with an eagerness in his eyes as he saw my cock. I let him play with it for a few minutes.

I laid back on the bed and had him straddle me on his knees above my face with his ass facing me. His ass looked beautiful! I had him lower himself as he lowered his balls into my mouth. I sucked on his nuts as he reached down and stroked my throbbing cock.

Then, he fell completely down on my chest and leaned all the way over to suck my cock. He knew his business as his lips moved over my hard cock. This guy was giving me the best head I had ever had. It took me a minute to catch my breath.

I then realized what a great position he was in. His ass was pointing directly at me. I licked from his balls to his ass. I let my finger play with his tiny opening. He had an ass like I had never seen before. I knew I had to have it. I let my tongue lick up his crack a few times. His ass started to shake and he began to moan. His cries were muffled by my hard cock which was still sliding in and out of his mouth.

I pulled him up and slid out from underneath him. He knew exactly what I wanted as he got on all fours and pointed his ass at me. "Fuck me, Mike!" he begged.

I moved in and grabbed his hips. His ass was shaking with anticipation again. I pulled his ass cheeks apart and took aim.

"Yeah, do it!"

I pushed my cock into his small opening and let out a cry. He was so tight and smooth. He cried out too as I slowly began to pump in and out. We soon got our motions together and were working like a machine. His ass moved back to meet my approaching cock. The bed was shaking under our forceful motions. Soon I felt myself start to come. I reached around him and grabbed his cock and stroked it as I neared.

I let out a loud cry as I shot my load into Jake's ass. He came again and started to shoot onto the bed. We fell forward, me on top of him. I left my cock buried in him as we recovered. After a few minutes, I slowly withdrew. His ass was now slick with my cum. He moaned again as he felt my cock slide out of him.

We lay next to each other for a long time. We drank some more wine and stayed lying next to each other on the bed. It didn't take long for him to recover. Jake reached for my cock and I looked down and smiled as I saw his growing erection. He moved close up to me and pressed his penis into mine while he reached for my ass. He started to grind his hips into me as he let his fingers play with my crack. I guess it was my turn this time.

He moved his fingers away and replaced them with his cock. The tip was soaked with slick pre-cum. I moaned softly as he rubbed his dick along the crack of my ass.

"Lean back, just a little," Jake said.

I twisted my head around and nibbled at his nipples. I bit them ever so softly and reached behind me to rub his balls. His cock was still in the crack of my ass, and I could feel the juices slowly lubing my tight hole.

With one quick thrust, he was inside me. The pain was so intense and I felt like I was going to faint. My back went rigid and my body started to shake. Neither of us moved for what seemed like an eternity.

"Relax," Jake said, "I'll go slow."

Even after all the beer I'd had, I was completely sober, now. This wasn't quite what I'd had in mind for this encounter, but there was no turning back now, as he started to slowly pump that huge piece of meat inside me.

Jake grabbed my ass cheeks and pulled them further apart, at the same time lifting me up just a little, so he could get a little more room to pump.

I'd never felt anything like this before. Amazingly, my cock was still hard. He thrust further inside me, and I could feel the tip of his cock hitting my prostate. I felt like I was going to explode, faint, and cum at the same time. His thrusts quickened and deepened. Involuntarily, my body moved in time with his. Deeper and deeper he went, and it seemed he'd found a magic place inside me.

Jake's breathing was shallow and his face started to turn red. I couldn't hold back anymore and shot my load all over his chest and face. It just kept coming. Load after load, as if I hadn't come for months instead of just hours. I'd completely forgotten about the pain, because it felt so good!

He pulled me down on top of him, forcing the root of his cock all the way inside me. Somewhere in the distance, I heard him groan. I could feel everything that had been pent up inside him come bursting out and fill me up inside. He thrust and exploded again. Oh, it felt so good!

We sat like that, with him still inside me, for a few more minutes. Slowly, he pulled out. I couldn't move. I was paralyzed and shaking.

He reached up to my face and caressed my cheek.

"Now that wasn't so bad, was it?" he asked.

"God no, it was fucking amazing!"

I climbed off him and staggered into the bathroom to clean up, and then I walked back to the bedroom. Jake was pulling off the condom he'd put on without me noticing.

"You were great," he told me.

"Thanks."

"We've got to do this again sometime."

"Yep, I'm game."

"Good. I'll watch for you online then."

1 Mister Saturday Night

The summer rain lashed with full fury outside our house. I looked at the dark skies above. If they were of any indication, we were going to have more seriously rough weather.

I looked at the time again. It was almost six in the evening, and Fred was still not back home. Damn it! I thought. Where is he? Why did I love this guy so much? It was so unusual of him to be so late. It must be the storm, I thought. He and Dan must be held up somewhere. But then why did he not call with his mobile? Man, the rains were still not showing any signs of abating. I was getting so worried about Fred.

Then a car pulled into the driveway.

Dan's Cavalier.

The two of them got out of the car and ran for the house—I had the door open and waiting for them to dash through without slowing. "Now where have you been so long? I was getting worried."

"It's the fucking rain," Dan cursed. "The stores were busy and it took forever to get through the line at the liquor store."

"And Dan left his cell at home, or I would have called you," Fred told me. "Sorry we made you worry."

I went over to the counter and quickly poured three run-and-cokes and handed them to the others.

Dan just gulped at his. "Damn, I needed this."

I took a good look at him.

Dan stood there in the doorway, dressed in his tight black Levis. He was always wearing tight clothing—and he'd had more than one blowout at work when seams gave way as he bent over—and he always looked good.

"So, boxers or briefs tonight?" Fred asked after we were on our second round of drinks of the evening.

"I'm going commando tonight," Dan said.

"Really?" Fred asked.

Without warning, I reached my hand down into the back of his Levis. "Yep," I announced as I gently squeezed his fuzzy ass cheeks. "He's not wearing anything under his jeans."

Dan laughed nervously.

"Well, you phoned us up wanting a night out with the guys," I told him, giving his ass another squeeze. "We do aim to please."

He nodded. "The wife's out with the girls. No reason I should stay at home all alone."

"None at all," we both agreed.

"More wine?" Fred refilled his glass.

I smiled and we exchanged looks. Dan was predictable. His wife would go out with her friends and he would be left alone and so he'd call us up to see what we were up too. Usually we were free. He'd come over, as eager as a puppy, have a few drinks to loosen up, and then we'd get his clothes off.

Speaking of which...I moved my hand around to the front of his jeans and that oh-so-impressive bulge. "Nice bulge going on here," I commented. I rubbed it slowly. "Mmm."

Dan moaned softly.

Fred walked over and ran his hand through Dan's recently trimmed beard. "Looking for more than just wine?" he asked. "As usual?"

Dan moaned again. The bulge in the front of his tight black jeans was getting really prominent.

I unzipped him.

His cock was already hard and it sprang into sight as soon as the zipper opened. No underwear to hold it in place after all.

"Very nice." I rubbed at it.

Dan pulled me close and kissed me. Our tongues rolled across each other and he moaned. I loved the feeling of his beard rubbing against my face.

Fred pushed me aside so that he could start kissing Dan. That was okay with me. I moved downwards to Fred's pants. I unzipped his fly, and then dragged his jeans down to his knees and began licking at his cock. He sprang to full attention almost instantly. I could see the naughty look on Fred's face and I could see his huge bulge underneath his undies. I gently kissed his briefs and pulled them down with my teeth. And there it was, his huge throbbing meat waiting to be sucked.

Wasting no time I got down to action. I first licked his hairy balls and then moved my way up. I moved my tongue upward to his dick, gently licking it from the sides. As I licked his throbbing dick small amounts of pre-cum oozed out of his dick. I licked them up greedily as I continued to please his dick.

Dan's hand reached inside my t-shirt and tweaked my right nipple. "Oh yeah," I moaned to him. Nipple play was one of my main weaknesses. "Just keep doing that."

Fred stopped kissing him long enough to pull off his shirt over his head.

We stumbled through the house to the staircase. The three of us were constantly touching and groping and kissing. My pants were left in the living room. My briefs were lost in the hallway. Fred's jeans were abandoned at the bottom of the stairs. His shirt came off in the bedroom.

Dan sprawled on the bed. Fred was kissing him, the two of them getting seriously hot and bothered. It was hot watching the two of them play with each other. Any other guy might be jealous, but not me. This was my fantasy too, and I was right there, playing along.

Fred straddled him, kissing him while rubbing his cock against Dan's. The friction made for some interesting sensations—I knew that from previous experience of my own.

There they were—lying on the bed. I looked at them with a smile on my lips. I really loved Fred, and I knew he loved me the same way. There was no one else on the earth that could make love to me like Fred did. It was like we were made for each other. Dan was a great friend, one of the first I had made when I started working at the warehouse, and we had the same tastes in movies, humor, etc.

If I wasn't already partnered with Fred, and if Dan was totally gay, then I might seriously have built a relationship with him.

I jumped onto the bed, by Dan's side. I gently ran my fingers over his hairy chest. I pinched his nipples and kissed them gently.

Fred moaned. Dan and I both knew all his 'pleasure points' and while I worked all over Dan's chest, his tongue was toying with Fred's nipples

Dan and I kissed again, our tongues exploring each other's mouths. We were lying side by side, embracing each other, lost in each other.

Dan could bare the excitement no more. He pushed my head right into his cock, asking me to suck it real hard. Dan kept pushing his dick further into my mouth till it was fully in.

Fred was running his hands along Dan's hairy chest, playing with the fur and sucking at his nipples with his tongue. Dan's eyes were closed.

I was sucking Dan now, working my mouth up and down along his cock. He was grunting and moaning. "Oh yeah, you could suck the chrome off a trailer hitch," he told me, his eyes closed in ecstasy.

"Oh ya! Suck harder!" Dan moaned. I continued to suck his man-meat. I paused for a quick moment and stole a look at his face and I could see that he was enjoying every moment of it. He continued to fuck my mouth pushing his dick in and out, gasping and moaning the whole time.

Within seconds he came, shooting his load in my mouth. I took my friend's cum in my mouth, sucking him real dry, not leaving a drop of his love juice.

By this time my dick was fucking hard. It was throbbing almost painfully. It was Dan and Fred's turn to explore me now.

They pushed me down to the bed and Dan kissed me deep, tasting his own cum. He knew all my pleasure points like I knew his. Man, I loved these guys. They knew how to make love. I had been with guys before Fred, but it was nothing like this.

Fred continued to lick my hairy chest with his tongue as I continued to enjoy every bit of it. He gradually moved down and stroked my dick with his beautiful hands as I moaned. Wasting no time he took my dick in his mouth.

He caressed it gently with his tongue and started to suck it real hard. He was one good damn cock-sucker. I could hardly control my ecstasy. Here I was with my lover and best friend, and there was nothing more wonderful in the world!

I grunted and then came in my lover's mouth as he readily swallowed every last drop of it. He swallowed as fast as I came.

We kissed each other again, lying side-by-side embracing each other. I felt like I was in heaven. It was like I wanted nothing else from this world than Fred to make love to me and be with me always.

The three of us kissed again. I could hear the thunder outside. I did not care. All that mattered was that both Fred and Dan were by my side. Nothing else really mattered.

I stroked Dan's rock-hard cock with my hand. *Still hard*? "We haven't gotten the edge off you yet, have we?" I asked.

"Fuck no." Fred and he were kissing. "Leanne just hasn't been in the mood lately."

I took a firmer grip. "We can't have that." I gave his dick a tug.

"Harder," he moaned.

I stroked him harder and more rapidly. I took a firm grip on his cock, like I used on my piece of meat, and stroked it.

A violent shudder wracked Dan's frame and he then came, shouting out with the force of his orgasm. He pumped out splash after splash of thick white cum which splattered across his hairy chest.

We lay in the bed, exhausted.

"I should get going," Dan announced. "She'll be home soon."

"You can always phone her," I offered. "Just leave a message on the machine for her. Spend the night here and we can have another session of serious *male bonding* in the morning."

He looked tempted for a long moment, and then reluctantly shook his head. "No, I should get going. Got a lot planned for tomorrow." He climbed out of bed and looked around for his pants.

"They're down in the kitchen I think." Fred laughed.

"You guys are so good, you make me forget where I left my clothes." Fred shrugged.

"Cum again sometime," I told him.

Dan just laughed and shook his head.

Running Hot

Dan pulled his car into the driveway with the customary squeal of tires. He pulled to a stop and got out of the green *Cavalier*. "Hey, Mike."

"Hi, Dan." I straightened up from the flowerbed I was trying to weed. At the moment, it seemed to be a lot more weed than flower. "What's up?"

"Nothing much," he said.

"I can see that." I had to stop and stare after all.

Dan was dressed in a very skimpy outfit. He had the right body for it though and I was envious. A low-cut white tank top that showed off most of his hairy chest and tight—*very* tight—biking shorts which hugged his bulge in very flattering way. "I was just going down to the Bay Trail for little jog. Thought you might like to come along."

Well, I was looking to lose some weight, which was something he knew, so I nodded. "Sure. Sounds like fun."

"Bring some water for afterwards."

I headed inside the house to the kitchen. "There should be some bottles already chilling in the fridge," I told him. "Let me go and get changed."

"Wear comfortable shoes," he told me. "Not sandles."

"Well duh!" I replied. "I figured that much out." *Give me some credit.*

I used the bathroom, then walked naked into the bedroom. I half-hoped to find Dan sprawled on the bed waiting for me to jump him, but I could hear him moving around downstairs. *Pity.* I pulled on a loose gray t-shirt and some green nylon shorts.

"You look really great in those shorts," I told him as the car pulled into one of the parking lots near the Bay. The Trail covered most of the waterfront and had numerous parks with ample parking. It was a nice place to walk or bike...I hadn't tried jogging along it yet.

"Leanne doesn't approve of them," he told me. "She thinks they're too tight for public viewing."

"Oh, I don't know about that. This particular portion of the viewing public appreciates them very much."

Dan laughed. "You're terrible."

"That's not what I usually hear in the bedroom."

He shook his head and gave his tank top a tug to try and shield his bulge. The effort was waste. "Let's get going."

"Okay."

We started jogging.

"Take it slow to start." Dan had shown me a few stretches and some quick muscle loosening techniques.

I could feel my legs shaking already. *I only just started out.* "I'm not sure how good I will be at this."

"You're doing fine." Dan was covering twice the distance I was. He would pull ahead twenty feet or so and then turn around and jog back to me.

I was barely keeping up with him. Still, the view from behind was quite nice and that kept me going. Dan had long legs and those shorts were stretched tight against his butt. He had a runner's build which I envied.

I had muscular legs, nicely shaped, but even in school I had lacked speed and stamina during sports. I could walk forever without complaint, and at a fairly brisk pace, but I couldn't run any distance to save my life.

Dan watched me stumble along. "Just find your rhythm."

"I have no rhythm," I gasped.

I was flagging and we had only just started out! Hell, I could barely spare the energy to look around at the other people enjoying the Bayside Trail. A pity, cause in addition to Dan, there were a number of extremely hot-looking people out. The day was warm and most of the guys were dressed in shorts and t-shirts. Many of the nicer specimens were even shirtless.

One hunky twenty-something was headed my way. Shirtless, his chest bronzed by the sun, he was wearing loose red nylon shorts. There was a nice sway in the front of his shorts as he jogged towards us. I even twisted my head around to watch him go past. "Hmm," I sighed. "Nice coming and going...and I'd really like to see him cumming."

"Pay attention."

I turned back towards Dan at the same moment I realized that I had slowed to a walk. "Sorry? You were saying?"

"Try to watch where you're going."

"This is harder than sex."

Dan laughed. "You're still working up an honest sweat." He didn't appear to have even broken one yet.

I walked the distance from lamppost to another and then managed to jog for two posts. Then I walked one and jogged two more. It worked for me.

Dan kept jogging, never slowing his pace. I envied him the ability to keep moving while I was barely staggering.

"You're doing fine," Dan told me. He was walking slow circles in a parking lot while waiting for me to catch up with him.

I stood in one place, gasping for air. "I'm exhausted."

"You're halfway done."

I stared at him. "Only *halfway*?" I was ready to drop.

"We have to jog back to the car you know."

"I'll just collapse here on the pavement and wait for you to bring the car to me." I offered him a weak smile. "Maybe I'll get mouth-to-mouth from a cute paramedic."

"He'd better have all his shots then."

My mouth dropped.

Dan laughed at my expression. "Hey, you give me shots like that all the time."

"True." I had to take them in return.

"Let's go." Dan set off at a steady pace.

I followed at a slow pace, almost staggering.

The eye candy was still nice, but I just didn't have the energy to keep up with him. I tried to focus on small things...the distance between lampposts. The approaching cyclist. The hot guy with no shirt wading in the Bay.

At last we turned into the parking lot from which we had set out what felt like hours ago.

"Don't stop cold. Do some more stretching so you don't get muscle cramps later on."

"I just want to drop."

Dan was doing some slow walking circles of his car. "Just relax."

"I suck at jogging," I panted as I unscrewed the top of the condensation wet plastic bottle and took a long swallow of cold water.

"You did fine for a first timer." Dan shrugged.

"I have no stamina."

"You did fine."

"I'm just not a runner."

"Hey, don't be so hard on yourself. And don't judge yourself by me. I used to run marathons."

I took another drink and waited for my heart to stop pounding.

Dan started up the car.

I walked into the kitchen. Dan honked as he backed out of the driveway onto the street.

"Dan not staying?" Fred asked me.

"He wants to go home and shower. We were jogging."

"He could have showered here."

"You wish."

"Yep."

"I just don't have the energy for that right now." My legs still felt like rubber. I eyed the water jug on the counter.

"Have fun?"

"Yes. Just two buddies out for some exercise. If I go out and do that often enough I might get a really good figure."

"I like your figure," he told me quickly. "You don't have Dan's torso, but your legs are better. I like the way you both look."

I looked at Fred. "Not every visit with Dan has to involve sex."

Fred shrugged. "He's not so clumsy when he's on his back."

"You're terrible."

"Want me to make you a drink?"

"Yes." Then I shook my head reluctantly. "Better not have alcohol right now," I told him. "Some fruit juice and a long soak in the tub is what I want right now." I staggered upstairs.

Good Job

I was painting the stair railing in my house. I was dressed in some pretty old clothes and had the house all to myself. I'd just pulled on some well-worn *Wranglers*, with frayed cuffs, gaping holes in the knees, and a small rip in the back seam. My green button-front t-shirt was loose and baggy. No point in wearing good clothes for messy painting, right?

"Hey, Mike!" There was a knock at the front door and Jake walked on in. I'd left the inner door open—to catch what breeze I could—so he could see me through the screen on the storm door. "What you up too?" he asked.

"Just trying to get the stairs looking good. Got my folks coming up on the weekend and I want this place to be ready." This would be their first time visiting at the house and I wanted everything to be perfect for them.

"Looking good," he told me.

"You're not looking at the railing, are you?" I asked.

"Nope." He had a big smile on his face. "Not at all."

"Don't you have to be at work?"

He just shrugged. "Not for a good hour." He loosened his tie and rested his hands on his hips. The navy blue dress pants he was wearing were fairly snug on his hips. "So where's Fred?"

"At work. My day off to enjoy the house. He gets the place to himself on Friday."

"Lucky you." He began to climb the stairs towards me.

I set the brush onto the paint tin and turned around.

Our lips met in a kiss.

"The bedroom's this way."

"I know." He pushed me up the stairs. "Oh, nice." He ran his hands along my ass. "This is the sight I like to see on the stairs."

I kissed him back and ran my hands along his dress shirt. Luckily for him I was clean...no paint on me at all. *Pity that, I was dressed to get messy and so far I was as clean as when I first got up.* I fumbled with the buttons on his shirt. The bulge in his pants was growing more noticeable. "Excited, aren't you?"

"Oh yeah." He reached up and ripped my shirt open, buttons flying from the collar as he ripped the cotton apart to get at my hairy chest.

"Mmm," I moaned as he nibbled at my now-exposed nipple.

"Yeah, you like that don't you? You like it when I'm rough with you?"

I ran my hands through his dark hair, then down to the lower portion of his shirt that was still buttoned. My fingers fumbled with them.

His hand rubbed the bulge in the front of my jeans. "You're getting really excited aren't you?" His hands moved to one of the small tears and pulled at it. Tearing the denim open, he reached in. "No undies?" he sounded surprised. "Even better."

I finished unbuckling his belt and unzipped him, dropping his own pants onto the floor. The front of his white *Calvins* were bulging with his hard cock.

We kissed again. I nuzzled my face through his hairy chest. Then he dropped down to his knees. He pulled the tear in my jeans wider, so that he could pull my cock out through it. He began sucking and I gasped with pleasure.

Both of us were now naked. We abandoned the rags of my clothes and left them scattered on the floor with his discarded suit, and we fell into bed. He lay on top of me, pressing me onto the mattress. Our hard cocks rubbed against each other as he moved his hips. "You like it a bit rough, don't you?"

"Yeah," I replied.

We kissed again—I'm such a sucker for a good kisser.

Jake moved his body. "You want some of this, don't you?" He brushed the tip of his cock across my lips.

"Oh yeah," I said. I licked the pre-cum from the slit. "Hell yeah." My lips opened and I took it inside my mouth. I licked it, playing with it while Jake moaned and thrust his hips in and out.

"I'm getting close!" He pulled out and held his cock just out of reach of my lips. "Not so fast...we don't want to rush things too much. Why waste the morning so quickly?" He kissed me passionately. I kissed back, our tongues sliding across each other.

We kissed each other while I stroked his hard cock. He was rubbing mine and we both grunted and moaned.

I stirred a bit and I felt the warmth of Jake's hands as he massaged down my back, moving closer to my firm butt. I moaned slightly, feeling the drool on my cheek, and giving in to the warm firm hands as hey massaged my lower back and then the top of the crack between my ass cheeks.

I instinctively spread my legs a bit and could hear Jake chuckle a bit. "Hi there, stranger," he whispered.

I replied with a contented, "Don't stop what you're doing."

He chuckled again, and reached between my slightly opened legs to stroke my balls. He ran a finger along the underside of my penis of my balls to the sensitive hole. I shivered and responded by pushing my hips up higher.

Jake replaced his finger with is tongue and licked around my puckered hole. That always drove me wild and now I was nearly fully awake, my own hard shaft trapped between my belly and the damp bed sheets. I ground it into the bed as he wet my hole. I could feel Jake's own hard-on against my calf, moving as he dry humped my leg.

Jake reached over and slid a condom off the nightstand and placed it on his own rod. I guess he must have had quite a sight as he sat on his knees over

me. My ass was there, slightly raised. He reached in and spread my legs apart further and slid between them. He ran his hands down the insides of my thighs and I was completely full of lust.

"Please, fuck me, Jake," I managed to croak out.

Jake laid on top of me, his rod in my crack. He slowly eased it to its target and then I could feel the head breach the mark. It slid in easily and I could hear him gasp. I moaned and pushed back, causing him to impale me further. Soon, he was completely inside me. He paused, enjoying the feeling and allowing me to become accustomed to him. Then, he started slowly moving his hips.

Just an inch or two moved in and out of me. But after a while, I pushed myself up onto my knees. He started sliding his hard cock in and out of me completely while I stroked my raging dick. Grunting with his every push, I was happy to please Jake. His breathing became irregular, and I lay back down on my stomach.

He popped out of me when I lay quickly down. Jake started to protest, but he soon smiled when he saw me roll over onto my back. I spread my legs apart and grabbing his latex covered rod, I directed it back to my waiting hole.

He plunged in quickly this time and I gasped as he breached me. I ran my hands over his hairy chest as he found his rhythm. His back was arched and the look of ecstasy was delicious as he gave himself over to the desire in him. With one free hand I stroked my aching dick and it wasn't long before I started gasping for air. He rocked me hard and my hand worked fast over my dick.

Then I convulsed, sending spray after spray of cum onto my belly and across Jake's chest.

Jake looked down as I rubbed the white gooey mess into his chest hair and tweaked his hard nipples. He wasn't smiling anymore. His eyes were glazed and he drooled, just a little. He started pushing, not so regularly now. I knew it wasn't long, and I pinched his right nipple hard and squeezed my ass with all my might. He was stuck and then he shuddered, spraying his thick cream deep in me. I milked him and he squirmed as I squeezed until he begged me to stop.

I relaxed enough for him to pull himself out. He tugged off the goo-filled condom, and then shuddered. "Oh fuck!" Jake gasped. "Oh fuck yeah!" His eyes closed as he began to cum a second time, without further stimulation. Thick white strands splattered across my chest.

That was all the encouragement I needed. I began to shoot a second load of my own, totally unexpected on my part, crying out from the force of the orgasm.

Then Jake collapsed onto my chest with a shuddering gasp and we lay there, gasping for breath.

"That was amazing," he said.

"I know."

"You give great head."

I laughed.

We lay in the bed.

"Shit, is that the time?" Jake jumped up and fumbled for his clothes.

I stretched out. "Is that your style?" I asked him. "A quick fuck and then you run out?"

"When I'm late for work: yes." He tucked his shirt into his pants. "You were great."

"I've been told that."

He leaned over and gave me a quick kiss. "Later."

"Watch the paint on the stairs," I reminded him.

"I will." He chuckled. "Good job," he said with another smile.

Fishing Bait

Dan had a relative who owned a cottage over in the County, and who was away for a few weeks on business. Dan suggested that he and I should go out fishing in the Bay and I had agreed. We had the place to ourselves and made ourselves at home on the dock.

After a few hours of catching nothing but branches, boredom began to set in and we decided to call it quits. It was such a beautiful day, though, that we thought it might be nice to go for a hike. So we put our gear back in the cottage and hit the trails. It had to be close to thirty-five degrees that day and very humid. Dan had removed his shirt and the sight of his runner's body glistening with sweat in the hot sun, made my cock just about burst out of my shorts.

We walked for what seemed like miles, teasing each other by grabbing at each other's asses as we climbed over fallen logs and pushed through the brush. We came to a small hill and Dan was in front of me, his ass right in my face. I was thinking to myself how badly I wanted to fuck that tight ass of his. My cock was just about to explode! He reached the top and turned around to face me and I noticed from the bulge in his shorts he was thinking the same thing. He held out his hand to help me up and pulled me into him and gave me a deep kiss. I was on fire and I knew he was too. I let my hand slowly run across his sweaty muscular back down to his ass. His hand fell to my crotch and began to slowly massage my cock through my shorts.

"We shouldn't be doing this," he said.

"Of course we shouldn't." I kept kissing him though and he kissed me back. Then I pulled my head away. "We can stop any time you like."

"Well, there's no one around here but us," he said as he rubbed my hard, throbbing cock through my green nylon shorts.

"That's right, stud," I replied with a hungry smile. "Let's do it...I want your cock."

We were getting hotter and if something didn't happen quickly we would both cum in our shorts. Where we were standing really would not be all that comfortable for us to enjoy so we decided to look for a clearing of some sort. We walked maybe a hundred feet and we found the perfect spot right next to the Bay, more like a marsh really. The grass was low and soft and it led to a rather muddy bank. Anyway I couldn't take it anymore. We stood in the grass and I dropped to my knees and unzipped his khaki shorts to unleash his cock. I was so fucking horny that I just gobbled it up and gave him the sloppiest juiciest blowjob I could. He began to moan in ecstasy, as I ravaged his thick eight inches. I loved Dan's cock.

Of course, he claimed to be straight, with a wife, but we fooled around with each other a lot and we both loved cock. Sucking it, getting fucked by it and especially getting a hot load of cum outta it and I planned to do all three!

My cock-sucking was becoming too much as he pushed my head away. "Slow down man! I don't want to cum yet."

"Oh you're gonna cum...you're gonna cum all over my face, all over my chest, all over my cock, all over my ass..."

Dan began to laugh as he stroked his cock. "All over your ass huh?"

"Yeah all over it," I repeated. "I want your cock in my ass."

He chuckled. "Get those shorts off... you slut."

I got up off my knees took off my sneakers and slipped out of my shorts. It felt so good to be outside in the sun completely naked.

Dan on the other hand was having some trouble. He tried to slip his shorts over his shoes. It was hilarious...he got one sneaker off and one leg off but he couldn't get the other one. So he was hopping on one foot with a raging hard-on, trying to tug his other shoe and the shorts off. I just couldn't stop laughing, and I saw it coming. Just as he got them off watch out I yelled a warning.

"Oh shiiiiii......SPLAT!!!!"

Dan landed right on his ass in the mud. I was dying now. He just sat there naked in the mud, holding his shorts with the shoe stuck in it. His

frustration subsided and he began to laugh as well. "What I go through for some cock, huh?" he complained as he laughed.

As my own laughter subsided I began to notice how sexy he looked.

His arms and shoulders were covered, as were most of his legs. The mud had splattered over the rest of his body, but what I distinctly remember was that his legs were spread and the mud began to seep up to his balls and his hard-on. It looked so hot. He took his muddy hand and began to stroke his cock and he began to rub the mud all over his chest with his other hand. He began to moan. "Oh man...this feels great!"

And it looked great.

"Come on, Mike, get in here...if you want to get fucked, then you're getting dirty too."

"Ha! Is that so?" I replied. "Then I guess I have no choice." I took a running leap and did a belly flop—or should I say a hard cock flop?—into the mud, right next to Dan.

"All right, I give it a ten, and that ass a ten." Dan rolled over and buried his face in my ass. The sensation of him licking my ass and the feeling of my cock in the mud was incredible. I began to fuck the mud! Dan stopped and picked up a handful of mud and plopped it right on my ass. It felt wonderful as it seeped through the crack of my ass. He picked up another one and it landed right on my head.

"What the hell?" I said in mock sarcasm. I rolled over and he fell off laughing. We began to wrestle around getting ourselves completely covered, massaging it in each other, stroking each other's cocks with our muddy hands. The mud, which was once thick and goopy, was now silky smooth from all the churning. Kinda like chocolate pudding and it felt wonderful.

Dan straddled my chest and jokingly said, "Suck my dirty cock, bitch."

"What the hell," I told him, and to his surprises I stuck his muddy cock in my mouth. It tasted awful and I gagged a bit...but I spat it out (as the saying goes) and before long his cock was clean. He began fucking my face and I could hear the mud squishing around my head. If I didn't slow down he was gonna cum and I wanted that cock in me! I stopped sucking and looked up at his muddy face and told him to fuck me.

A big white smile appeared through the mud and he slithered down my body and lifted my legs up so as to get my asshole out of the mud. It was difficult at first because we kept sliding around but finally he positioned it right at my bud and with my knees close to my head, he slid it in to the hilt.

I let out a grunt. "Ungh. Oooh yeah...that feels awesome. Fuck my ass man."

Dan began moaning and fucking me harder, even managing to hit my prostate. He was fucking me hard...and I was loving it!

He began to fuck me furiously...squishing sounds filled the air...and mud began splattering up around us. He began to moan. "I'm gonna cum dude...I'm gonna cum!" A few more thrusts and he pulled out and jerked his load all over my stomach, chest, and face. The mixture of cum and mud was quite interesting to look at. Almost like a painting.

He began laughing.

"Hey," Dan said, "that's not fair. I haven't gotten fucked yet!" He jumped off me and got on all fours in the mud. "Stick your cock in my ass...I want a muddy fuck too."

I was happy to oblige. I entered him with ease and began pounding his ass. Dan sat up with my cock still in him and turned his head around to tongue my muddy mouth. As we were tonguing each other, I reached around and stroked his muddy cock with my equally muddy hand. We started going at it real hard in that position. Mud was flying everywhere. I found myself slipping backward then...Splat!

I fell backwards my ass and back in the mud with Dan on top of me still riding my cock. He leaned all the way back on top of my chest and turned to kiss me again. I noticed over his shoulder, his mud covered cock glistening in the sun was hard again and oozing pre-cum. He then suddenly sat up and with me still inside him turned around to face me. He was close to coming again and I was close to cumming for the first time that day. He began to ride me furiously. He was bouncing up and down on my cock, mud was flying everywhere, his groaning becoming more frequent, and his riding more urgent.

"Oh shit man...I'm gonna cum again...ughh!" Another load shot out of his cock painting my mud-covered body with his jizz.

I still had not cum yet and being the good man that he is, Dan continued to ride my cock.

"Come on man...cum for me. That's it. Cum for me." He continued his furious ride while cheering me on. It didn't take long.

"Oh that's it, Dan. I'm cumming...."

He jumped of my cock and slithered down just in time to take my load in his mouth.

We spent most of the rest of the afternoon in the mud. We fucked each other some more, played around, and just lay there enjoying the luxurious feeling of the mud covering our naked bodies before finally heading back to the cottage to clean up.

Kung Fu Who

Dan and I had been friends for several years now. We both worked in the same department in a large warehouse. We hung out a lot, with his wife and with Fred. But we spent a lot of time as just the two of us.

I'd gone over to Dan's house one evening to watch some samurai movies. Fred had chosen to stay home—he had no interest in poorly dubbed and equally poorly acted *chop suey* flicks—but Dan and I loved the genre. To make the movies more watchable, we were drinking a good number of rum-and-cokes. Nothing like *Captain Morgan* and kung fu to make an evening fun.

We were seated on the couch, comfortable and relaxed. Even Dan's wife had chosen to vanish for the evening, off for a girl's night with her younger cousins.

Dan paused the movie to rave about the latest martial arts star.

I made a passing comment that he was over-rated.

Dan stood up, towering over me with his six foot three height.

I matched my five-and-a-half foot frame with his. I commented that Dan wouldn't know a good martial arts movie from a fortune cookie. That might have been the wrong thing to say, but we'd both had a fair amount to drink. More than enough to quash our usual inhibitions.

Dan reached over to me and grabbed me by my t-shirt collar and just ripped it down the front of his chest, exposing my hairy chest and pecks.

I was pretty startled by having my tee ripped open so suddenly, and a little ticked cause that red *Nike* was one of my faves. Without even thinking what I was doing, I grabbed Dan's *Reebok* tee shirt by the back of the sleeve and pulled it toward the center of his chest, causing it to rip apart at the sleeve, shoulder, and down the side.

"So there," I told him.

He looked back at me.

Dan was in very good shape. He had a light coat of brown hair covering his chest and arms. He had a definite runner's build. I knew that he was a runner and he had the build for it.

Both of us lunged at each other and immediately fell to the carpet, thrashing around. We made for quite a sight, I'm sure, drunkenly wrestling with each other. Eventually, Dan ended up on the bottom, sprawled face down on the floor. I was sitting on top of him, straddling his back.

I took hold of one of the back pockets on Dan's jeans and tore it clean off. This tore the *Levis*, and exposed Dan's red *Hanes* briefs, and a well-toned leg. I was surprised at how easily the denim on those jeans tore.

Dan seemed surprised by the sudden draft on his backside. "Oh yeah?" But then he managed to reach around and grab the front pocket on my corduroy slacks. With one swift motion he pushed me off-balance and we both heard the thunderous *RIPPPPP*. I fell over and my slacks were torn down the outside seam from the pocket to well below the knee.

Both of us were quick to get back on our feet. Again we lunged at each other. Dan grabbed my other front pocket and spun me around very hard and fast. The shear force of this caused my cords to completely rip down the other side, and up through the waist. My brown cords immediately fell into a pants' puddle around my ankles, leaving me standing there in my crisp gray cotton briefs. I was getting aroused at this point, but hoped Dan did not notice.

Of course, Dan could not fail to notice the growing bulge in my briefs, but he said nothing because he was getting aroused himself! Those tight clothes he favored left little to the imagination.

I quickly removed my other leg from the torn cords, tossed them aside, and then went after Dan wearing just my gray briefs and torn t-shirt. I did give one brief thought as to the neighbors, but the blinds were drawn. Screw the neighbors, I wanted Dan and I wanted him now! I grabbed Dan and bear-hugged him around his slender waist. Then with a grunt, I reached around and pulled the other back pocket off his jeans.

The back of Dan's jeans was now completely torn wide open. In these close quarters, I could now feel that Dan also had an erection. This made me even hotter, knowing that both of us were getting turned on. I pushed Dan backward, causing him to land hard on the couch. I bent down in front of him and grabbed what remained of Dan's jeans by the closure and zipper.

"You wouldn't," he began.

"I would." I gave one huge tug, and with loud *rip*, Dan's jeans were splayed open from his waist, breaking the zipper, and torn through the crotch and down the inner thigh seams of the jeans past his knees.

By now it was impossible for either of us to hide our erections, and we both knew that we were enjoying ourselves. Besides admiring Dan's ample erect dick that could not be restrained by his red briefs, I was impressed by the shape Dan had kept himself in. He had a washboard stomach, and great abs, along with nice legs.

I needed a better look so I proceeded to rip what remained of Dan's *Levis* off, and threw them aside. I then got down on top of Dan and started grinding him, with some serious cock-on-cock action through our briefs. Dan was going to explode!

He knew he had better do something fast or it was all going to be over. Dan carefully exposed my cock and balls through the fly of my briefs, and started to rub and massaging them in order to get my weight off him. Dan had seen me naked often enough and he knew just how well endowed I was.

I was really enjoying having my cock and balls rubbed and massaged. I started to raise his body off Dan, so that Dan could continue with the massage. Dan had other plans though. When my body was up just enough, Dan stopped the massage, and grabbed my gray cotton briefs by the fly, and pulled at the opening. My crisp briefs gave out with one continuous *RIPPPPP*, and were completely torn off my body, leaving just the waistband intact.

I immediately stood up; my cock had never been stiffer or straighter. It almost hurt. I starred down and saw the inability of Dan's briefs to restrain his own stiffened cock. I reached down, and took one side of the *Hanes* briefs and just pulled on them as hard as I could. *RIPPPPP*. Dan's red briefs were shredded off his body and in my hand. I put the red briefs up to my face, in order to get the full aroma of Dan. I then looked down at Dan to see my handy work and admire Dan's throbbing dick. "You've shaved recently."

"Yep, right down to the wood."

"Nice." I ran my hand through the stubble.

Tossing the red briefs aside, I knelt down on the floor, and put my head in Dan's crotch, taking Dan's erect cock into his mouth. Dan reciprocated by taking my throbbing cock and stroking it. We had a great rhythm going, until neither of us could take it any longer. We both exploded at the same time and his cum overflowed my mouth and dribbled into my goatee.

After both of us could not cum anymore, we just lay there on the floor for what seemed like an eternity.

Still in our torn tee shirts, I finally said, "I'm exhausted".

To which Dan replied: "What was the argument about?"

"I don't remember any more."

"We need to wrestle more often!"

"I'm gonna need to borrow something to wear home."

Dan just laughed.

Bargain Buy

"Thanks for coming out with me," Dan commented.

"Any time," I replied. The mall was crowded, but that was expected this close to Christmas. I shoved my hands into the pockets of my nylon pants.

"I'm never sure what to get her. She doesn't need any more perfume. I can't afford jewellery right now."

"Ah, the trials of shopping for the ball-and-chain," I chuckled.

Dan gave me a dirty look.

I chuckled and adjusted my dark green scarf, to give myself a more jaunty air. It was winter and I liked the feel of a scarf around my neck. My grandmother had knitted it for me when I was just a child and I still wore it. The color matched my bomber jacket.

We wandered around to *The Body Shoppe*.

"Something scented?"

"You'll have to tell me how it smells." Dan shrugged. "You know."

"Yep." An unfortunate childhood accident with a squirt of bleach had left Dan's sense of smell permanently lost. "This is nice." I inhaled the shampoo. "Very feminine."

The clerk came forward with other samples.

Dan was eying her.

A twenty-something in a tight top and pants. I wondered if she was for sale like the rest of the stock in the store. She was pretty, but did not do anything for me. No fire in my loins. I acknowledge that she was nice to look at, but I had no desire to sleep with her.

Dan was staring at her, almost drooling.

I snuck a glance at his crotch. The bulge in his tight blue jeans was there, as usual, but nothing overly pronounced.

Eventually the sale was made and we left the store.

"How about some chocolate?"

"Dan, I love you."

We headed for the mall's chocolatier and Dan treated me to a fine truffle. It was truly exquisite and I savored every small bite.

"I would have sex with anyone who offered me chocolate," I told him after he asked if I had enjoyed it.

"I've heard that about you," was his reply.

I eyed one passing college-aged guy. Brown leather bomber, tight jeans, loose green t-shirt...he looked as delicious as the chocolate.

"You're terrible!"

"What?"

"Drooling over that guy."

"So?" I countered. "You were drooling over the clerk."

Dan looked abashed. "I'm married; not dead." He gave the hem of his sweater a tug.

"Exactly." I laughed. "Straight men are all alike."

"*You* are a total horn dog."

"Yep." I gave him one of my best shit-eating grins. "It's one of my many strengths." Cruising the mall was one of Fred and my ideas of cheap entertainment. Pick the right night and the place could be packed with a throng of cuties...of course, some nights were a total bust in terms of eye candy.

We pulled out of the parking lot and onto the street.

Dan took the corner faster than I would have. He moved the gearshift like he handled me in the bedroom. Hard. "I think I need to get the stick looked at. It feels a little stiff."

I looked at him. "Really?"

"Yeah."

My eyes rested on his crotch. "It does look a little stiff from here."

"What are—" his eyes tracked my line-of-sight. "Never mind."

"Never mind?" I repeated. I reached over and rested my hand on his knee. "Are you sure?"

He mumbled something.

I moved my hand higher up his leg.

We pulled into the driveway.

"Do you have to rush back home?" I asked. "Or can you come up for a bit?"

"I can stay for a while. Leanne is working late tonight."

We got out of his car. While he paused, I unlocked the door. "Fred's not home yet."

"Lucky him."

"Lucky us. We got the day off to enjoy. He had to work." I hung up my jacket and then took Dan's leather coat away from him. It smelled like his cologne. "It was fun going to the mall with you."

"I was glad you were there. Leanne is gonna love the soaps."

"She's going to smell very nice. Very fruity."

Dan chuckled.

"Can I offer you something?" I asked. "A drink?"

"Something hot would be nice."

"Tea?" I filled the kettle and plugged it in. "The coffee jar is up on the top shelf." Out of my reach—Fred and I couldn't stand the taste of coffee, but we kept a small jar for guests. "It should only take a few minutes."

Dan was standing near the patio doors and stretching. He had his back to me and his jeans were stretched tightly across his buttocks.

"Hmm mm," I commented.

Dan turned. "What?"

"Just admiring the view."

"You guys do have a wonderful backyard. I hope to get some serious work done on mine next year."

"That wasn't the scenery I was admiring, Dan." I took a step towards him. "Yes, we do have a nice yard...but the scenery in the kitchen is even nicer to look at.

"Oh." He looked me up and down.

I stepped close to him and gave him a kiss. He returned it.

"If you don't want to do this, we can stop," I told him. "Don't ever feel pressured."

"I want too." Dan rested his hand on the front of my pants. He stroked my growing erection through the black nylon. I was getting hard, no doubt about it. "I want too."

"Good. I want to too." I unzipped his jeans and pulled his cock through his briefs. I licked the tip of it, teasing him.

"Let's head up to the bedroom."

"Okay." I led him through the doorway with my hand still on his cock.

We moved into the living room...and got no farther.

The fire was burning brightly in the gas fireplace and Dan and I stopped to kiss again. We stood there, groping each other and kissing for long minutes, then we slowly sank down to end up laying on the carpet in front of the fire, still kissing and touching each other.

His sweater was tossed aside and I pulled his jeans down towards his ankles. My t-shirt was hanging off one chair and my nylon pants provided no more resistance to him than my *Hanes* briefs.

Dan nibbled at my nipples. He knew that was something I loved having done to me. I moaned.

I kissed him and he kissed back.

My hand ran through his hairy chest.

I went down on him, taking the full eight inches of his cock into my mouth. I made full use of my tongue and lips to give him a good time.

"Oh god!" Dan cried out. He started to buck his hips and I lost my grip on his cock. Cum shot from his rod, splattering across my groin in long ropy spurts.

"Oh yeah!" I said. I dropped a hand down to my own cock and used his cum as lubricant. In mere seconds, I was shooting my own sticky goo onto Dan's chest.

I collapsed into his arms.

"Wow."

"Wow indeed." I dabbed at his chest with my briefs. "We're a mess."

"Yeah. You are amazing."

"I've been told that."

"Now how about that coffee?"

"What did I miss?" Fred asked as he walked into the kitchen later that afternoon.

"Nothing much. Dan and I went shopping at the mall. You missed seeing Leather Boy."

"Mike was helping me get a few things for Leanne."

Fred nodded as he hung up his jacket.

"There's fresh tea," I offered.

"Sounds good." Fred smiled. "See anyone hot at the mall beside Leather Boy?"

"Yes."

"Damn."

"Maybe you'll have better luck later."

Just A Trim

"Dan's coming over. He needs a haircut."

"Just him, or is Leanne coming too?"

"Just him, I think."

"Woo hoo!" Dan came over for haircuts every few months. He liked the way that Fred cut his hair...and the *haircuts* had almost always led to more. Like naked fun in the bedroom. Well, Dan was usually shirtless for the cutting so getting his pants off as well wasn't too much of a stretch.

Dan walked through the door. A black leather ball cap covered his hair, and it matched the leather jacket.

"Well *hello* leather boy!" I called from the couch.

"Hello yourself." Dan tossed his jacket on the back of a dining room chair. "How's things?"

"Good. Too much work." I had worked overtime that morning and was still exhausted. I wasn't sure if I'd have the energy for Dan or not...but my cock twitched in my nylon pants as he sauntered into the living room. He always had that effect on me.

He looked hot in his clothes. Black *Wranglers* were tight against his legs and his butt and he was wearing an *Old Navy* sweatshirt.

Fred joined us with rum-and-cokes and we talked about what we had been up too recently. Mostly working, minor home renovations, and shopping.

"I had to buy some new jeans. They keep tearing in the crotch."

"Look at what the crotch is holding," Fred said.

"You wear your clothes too tight," I told him.

"I have the ass so why not flaunt it?" he asked boyishly.

"True." I nodded. "You have a very nice ass."

"How about that haircut?"

Fred and Dan headed upstairs.

I followed.

Dan removed his sweatshirt and sat on the chair. Fred already had the scissors and comb ready.

"Sure, I've been bitching for a week about getting my haircut and he keeps putting me off," I grumbled. "Dan calls up and 'Sure, come right over'! Hardly right."

"Well, he just has sex with you," Dan pointed out.

"And he likes it." Fred ran a hand across Dan's hairy chest.

I went to the bedroom to turn up the radio. Then I picked up the digital camera and turned it on. *Too good a chance to miss.*

I stepped around the corner and snapped a picture. Dan was sitting shirtless on a chair with Fred cutting his hair. "A great shot."

Dan shook his head.

"You're done."

"You look great." The short hair set off Dan's features much better than the ragged shaggy look.

"I need a broom." Fred headed downstairs with a still-shirtless Dan.

I was turning off the radio when I heard Fred ask: "Are those silk?"

"Yep, my *Scoobies*."

I shot downstairs and caught up to them in the kitchen where Dan was complaining that everything was in the laundry. "Silk boxers, Dan?"

"Yep." He pulled his waistband up so I could see more.

"That's hardly showing them off. Let me see those." I reached for his fly and fumbled with the zipper.

"Get away from there." Dan pulled away, and for a moment I wondered if I had gone too far too quickly, but then turned his back to us and unzipped his fly. He shoved his *Wranglers* down to his knees.

"Wow!"

The black and red *Scooby Doo* boxers looked great against Dan's legs. He did have a wonderful body.

"Quick," I said, "get the camera!"

Dan laughed.

Fred went back upstairs with the broom to sweep the hair off the floor.

"That looks really nice." I reached for the fly. It was unbuttoned. "You've already got a semi." I was stroking it through the opening.

Dan's eyes were half-closed. He didn't offer any complaints or objections, so I continued stroking him. "Want to head back up to the bedroom?" I asked him.

"Mmmm."

I rubbed against him, enjoying the feeling of his goatee against my cheek. "It's been a while since we had any fun."

"Yeah."

I dropped to my knees and starting sucking him.

He gasped.

Fred walked into the kitchen. "How're you two doing?"

"We're doing good." Dan could barely talk.

I stood up. "We're both doing good." The front of my nylon splash pants were bulging out.

Fred rubbed it. "Wow." He took hold of Dan's cock. "Wow," he repeated.

"Shall we adjourn to the bedroom?" I asked.

"Fuck yes," Dan said.

"Lead the way," Fred told him.

Dan pulled his *Wranglers* up and headed for the door.

They got to the bedroom first while I stayed downstairs to lock the doors behind us—it would be our luck to have his wife drop by to check up on him!—and headed upstairs to strip. Dan and Fred were both already naked, standing there kissing.

I moved to join them. I stepped up behind Dan, my erection sliding under his buttocks to rub against his balls. He gasped, but didn't stop kissing Fred. My hands reached around to their front, to rub Fred's nipples. They were getting very hard.

Fred moaned. "Mmm, a nice sight. A Dan sandwich."

Dan turned around and we kissed. His tongue went deep into my throat.

We were kissing and Dan was touching me freely. His hand was wrapped around my cock and he was stroking me.

We stumbled over to the bed.

I was kissing now, being aggressive.

Fred was performing oral on Dan, sucking his leaking cock.

Dan was stroking me, his hand rubbing my dick with fast strokes. It felt wonderful.

Dan's eyes had rolled back into his head and he could barely moan.

As Fred continued to stroke him, Dan grunted and began to cum. It seemed like gallons and gallons were spurting over his cock. I rubbed his cock too and he jerked with orgasmic aftershocks.

My hand was coated with Dan's man-juice and I hastily rubbed it along my own member. Dan kissed me while Fred stroked my hard nipples and within moments, I was cumming.

Fred laid down with Dan and me both kissing him and stroking his cock.

Fred moaned and came, cum spurting over his hand.

"And like Austin Powers said, '*I'm spent.*'" Dan slumped onto the bed. "Gods, that was amazing."

"We have got to get some movie cameras set up in here," I commented. "This would make a fortune on the net."

Dan laughed. "I'd have to kill you then."

I Bet You Will

Dan was probably my best friend, aside from Fred. We had started placing bets with each other. Dan was into hockey and, even though I had next to no interest in the sport, we often made friendly wagers on the games: a mickey of rum, wash the winner's car, and do the winner's laundry were our typical bets.

Anyway, one Saturday night we were watching a hockey game in the living room of his house. We were both wearing gym shorts and T-Shirts. We were drinking rum-and-coke and being our normal cocky selves and Dan was insisting that the Leafs were going to win the game. I knew he was probably right but holding true to our friendship, I decided to aggravate him by insisting that the Penguins would win. We traded arguments back and forth for a while when I decided to offer the ultimate bet.

I suggested that we should place bets on the outcome of the game and that the loser had to be the winner's slave and perform any task for one hour. The only rule was that neither the winner nor the slave could ever speak of the bet to others and the payoff would be held in the strictest confidence. We both shook hands and settled in to watch the game. After the first quarter, the Leafs were up five nothing. Dan was feeling confident; at the half, much to my dismay, the Penguins had cut the lead to seven to four. The bottom line, it was a good second half, better than either of us thought but the Leafs won as expected.

The game was over and it was time to payoff. Dan didn't know exactly how to start but the heat in both of us was obvious. He decided to start by saying, "Slave, go to the kitchen and get me another drink."

I complied and waited for his next request.

Dan took a deep swallow from his drink and nodded. He smiled at me, a mischievous glint in his eyes. "Slave, take off your shorts and t-shirt."

I was then standing in front of him in just my Hanes briefs.

He could tell that I was beginning to get excited—the briefs left very little to the imagination. "Slave, on your knees!" Dan said.

I did so.

Dan got up and stood in front of me with his crotch inches from my face and then removed his shirt. "Slave, slowly remove my shorts", he ordered.

I carefully reached up and gently removed his shorts. I could see his cock begin to rise in his white Hanes briefs. He stepped closer to me, touching my face with his bulge. "Slave, remove my underwear, but only use your mouth," Dan instructed.

I couldn't believe what he was asking but I tried. I carefully grabbed the elastic band of his underwear in my teeth and began to slowly pull the front of his briefs off. The head of his cock touched my nose and I stopped in surprise. He was already beginning to drip pre-cum and a drop of it was smeared on the end of my nose. I had to move around to his backside and perform the same type of maneuver. His Hanes were now about half down and loose enough for me to grab the crotch of his underwear with my teeth and remove his underwear completely.

Dan stepped out of them and instructed me to resume my kneeling position in front of him. I knelt back down in front of him waiting for what I knew he would ask me to do.

"Slave! Lick your master's balls slowly."

I began to lick his sweaty nut sack. His cock was now seriously dripping pre-cum and hitting me on the forehead. I was beginning on my own to lick not only his nuts but also the base of his cock. Then I heard, "Suck my dick, boy!"

That was what I was waiting for! I opened wide and took as much of his hot throbbing cock as I could. I gently grabbed the remainder of his dick with my hand and slowly pumped it in my mouth. I could feel him begin to fuck my face. I sucked harder and he pumped faster. He began to thrust and then without warning I felt his hot nectar fill my mouth and run down my chin. He cried out—he was always noisy when he came. He spurted three or four times and then he began to relax. He slowly removed his cock and with his finger scooped the cum dripping from my chin back in to my mouth and lifted my chin to close my mouth. "Swallow my friend. Drink a little of my coke to wash it down. You have paid your debt well."

"Your turn is coming," I warned him.

Dan just laughed.

Lunch-Break

It was around half past twelve in the afternoon, and Jake was late. Not unusual for him, busy as he always kept himself in the real estate business. I don't think I've even stopped by his office, when he wasn't on the telephone talking with someone, while others waited on-hold, lined up like aircraft in a holding pattern waiting to land.

It wouldn't have surprised me to get a call from him, apologizing up and down, wanting to re-schedule for lunch, as he has so many times in the past. He knows me well enough to know I never mind it; it's the hazard of being successful. I figured I could put the time to good use while I waited, and pulled down a painting off the wall that I had been meaning to work on for a while. The frame needed a good cleaning, and after removing the artwork from it, I was polishing the frame edges when I heard a knock at the door. I stood up and looked out the dining room window; I could see it was Jake's car in the driveway.

I yelled out "It's open," and he quickly entered, looking a little flustered but sharp as ever. The guy knew how to dress; his taste in suits, choice of ties, et cetera, always impressed me.

Today was no different, one of his nicer summer suits, a navy single-breasted number, impeccably tailored, a tightly knotted red silk tie with gold fleck design, over his trademark crisp white-as-they-come cotton shirt, that contrasted so nicely with his deep tan. One thing about Jake; it could be 90 outside, but he always looked like he just stepped outside of an air-conditioned showroom. Except for that flush on his face today.

"What's the matter? You look a little frazzled today," I commented jokingly as he hurried past me into the den, dropping his briefcase on the dining room table with a thud.

"Oh, this cell-phone is acting up again," he grumbled. "I need to use your phone, fast. I was in the middle of closing a deal and was cut off in mid-sentence!" Before I had even finished saying the words "Of course", Jake had eyed the cordless phone on the tabletop, and made a leap for it. What he didn't notice in his haste was the picture frame I had been working on, laying against the table leg. One nail that hadn't been properly secured to the frame caught the leg of his slacks when he was leaning over it.

I yelled out, but it was too late.

Jake reeled back and looked down at his pants. "Oh fucking great! Look at this!" he barked. "I just ripped a hole in my pants! This day is going downhill real fast." Sure enough, halfway up his thigh, there was a clean cut in the material, running for about three inches.

I was quite upset; my first concern was that the nail might have cut him. "Are you ok? Did you get cut?" I asked, looking alarmingly at the tear.

He used his thumb to press against the rip, opening it up slightly more, exposing his leg. "No, I'm not cut," he stated without much concern. "Whatever that was didn't touch me, just the pants." He shrugged and went about his business like it was nothing, opening his briefcase up to retrieve his small personal phonebook, and then taking a seat in the chair to the side of the table.

I moved quickly to get rid of the frame, picking it up out of his way. "I am so sorry, Jake. It's all my fault; I really should have moved that frame somewhere else." I dropped it down against the wall. I made an offer to have the slacks replaced.

"Don't be silly," he laughed while dialing. "It's only a pair of slacks. Why look," and with that, he slipped his fingers inside the tear and ripped the material back even further, exposing another inch of flesh. "See?" he stated with a devilish smile, "it's not like a rip is the worst thing that can happen to a guy's suit."

My feelings immediately changed from one of concern to an excited interest.

He sat back in the chair, moving his legs slightly forward. I looked at the rip in his slacks; the opening exposed the skin on his leg. I could see how tanned his legs were, the pattern of dark hair on them, and it made me want to see more. His hesitation in dialing gave me the courage to say to him "In that case, hang up the phone...let's see where that rip leads."

Jake gave me the biggest grin, and hung up the receiver. I moved to his side, leaned down and placed my hand against his leg, rubbing along his inner thigh until my hand was just over the tear. I slipped my fingers inside of it, brushing the backs of them against his leg. "Your leg feels nice," I half-whispered to him, "but I don't think this rip is big enough, what do you think?" I looked into his cool-blue eyes, waiting for his response.

"I don't think so either," he said without pause, "but a word of warning." There was a hint of a smile on his face while he eyed my own white button-down shirt, his gaze running down the legs of my tan slacks and back up again. "I give as good as I take."

With the knowledge that all was fair game at this point, I decided to hold off on his slacks for the moment. I walked behind the chair that Jake was sitting in, looking down at him, his perfectly groomed jet-black hair, the spread of his shoulders, inhaling the scent of his cologne. I laid my hands on those broad shoulders; offering a short massage, the movement gaining strength gradually, pushing the collar of his jacket back, stretching it tighter and tighter, then sliding my hands over to the seams in the shoulders. Finely stitched...it would take a little work from this angle, unless I had a little help. "Jake," I asked in a sweet voice, "would you just open that box there on the table and hand me the scissors." They were just small fabric scissors, but sufficient for my needs.

Without a word, he took hold of the pair, passing them back to me. I made two very small cuts in the fabric, just along the shoulder seams. I leaned over him, laid the scissors back on the table, and stood back up, now able to slip the tips of my fingers under the openings I had just created, rolling the fabric over them in small circles, until they started to give way with the sound of shredding cotton fiber. Once I had all my fingers inside, rubbing against the lining, I pulled downward towards Jake, the sleeves of his jacket breaking free, now pushed down to his elbows, a few dark threads scattered along his white shirt.

He turned and looked at each arm, as if he approved of the changes, flexing his arms, watching the torn fabric gather. He pushed the chair back, away from the table, and stood up, facing me and leaning forward just far enough to get one of his hands around the back of my leg.

I stood perfectly still, while he slid his hand up and down my pant leg, finally stopping over the top of one of my back pockets. I could feel his grip tighten on it, and with one sharp tug, it ripped. He pulled down on it, past the pocket depth, continuing ripping halfway down the back of my leg. While I couldn't see it, I could feel the air against my skin, followed by his warm hand, rubbing where once the pants had been rubbing against me.

I was hot now, so hot I had to pull him to his feet in front of me. We stepped very close, and I ran my hands over one of the lapels, then over to the pocket top on his jacket. With one sure motion, I returned the job he did to the pocket on the back of my slacks, ripping the pocket down, pulling the white lining with it, letting it hang there.

Jake had started on my shirt, ripping one sleeve off, tearing it down to the cuff. He took hold of the front of my shirt with both hands, splitting it halfway down, the buttons on it breaking free, one of them bouncing off the tabletop before landing on the carpet.

I tore more into his jacket, the lapels, the side vents, anything and everything I could rip, until there wasn't enough left to stay on his frame; it just fell away.

My shirt was now in shreds. I could feel the collar still trying to hang on, and the cuffs were intact, but the rest was in several pieces laying down my pants, the tail of the shirt the only thing to keep that much on.

His shirt came off easy; reaching around the back collar, I ripped it downwards, pulling it forwards in two equal pieces on each side of him. It caught at the wrists, the bottoms there finally broke free on one of them, and I left his shirt hanging from the other wrist. I could see his nipples under his t-shirt, on two perfectly proportioned pecks.

"A very nice sight indeed," I murmured.

"I like what I'm seeing too," he replied.

I ran my hands down the center of them, down over his tight stomach, looking down at his slacks. I dropped to one knee, and he laid his hands on my shoulders, looking down, watching my every movement.

I found the original rip, and after slipping my fingers inside, tore the material down to the cuff, then ripped the opposite direction high up, making shorts out of one leg of them, a few inches higher up than the pocket lining now showing. Jake had on a pair of white cotton boxers with a light pinstripe that was showing, the dark hair on his upper leg patterning and disappearing up the leg vent on them.

I moved around him, ripping the seat out of his slacks, then the opposite pocket, ripped down to reveal more of his boxers. I came back around the front, and shredded the remaining pant leg into several long strands so when he moved his leg, they would slide around it.

Jake pulled me up, and I leaned back against the table as he tore into my slacks, ripping them to shreds in no time, until there was just the belted material under the waistband, and a thin line of material on each side of the zipper, that ran under my crotch to the back, still intact. I could feel the bulge in my white *Hanes* pressing against that zipper, his hands tearing away the last vestiges of my shirt, ripping my socks down to my shoes. Grunting, I grabbed his t-shirt, split it back, his hairy chest finally exposed to me, the material fallen over what was left of his shirt. I ran my hand down his chest, over the front of his slacks, still intact, until I grabbed hold of the side of them along the rip and pulled with such force, the belt loops gave way, sending what was left of them sliding down his legs to his knees.

Jake fell back against the chair, all that was left whole on him was his boxers...the rest of his outfit was in many pieces; some laying on the carpet, others trying to hang on to him. I moved my palm over the front of his boxers; I could feel the heat and the size and hardness of what was under them. I slid my fingers inside the loose fly; brushed them through his thick pubes, along the side of his hard shaft, then tugged, one last time. I was looking into his eyes, but I could feel the cotton of his boxers in my hand; they ripped off in one piece.

When I looked down, sure enough they were gone, his long thick cock rising upwards towards me, pulsing and throbbing. How he had made it this far without touching himself, I'll never know. I know how hard it was for me, but it was his touch I was waiting for...waiting for his hands to rip the back of my briefs open, to tear the front half of the fly, letting the material hang free, then ripping the sides forward, until there nothing but the band left.

I felt Jake slip his hands under the band, stretching the elastic outwards. He took hold of my cock, slid it up under it, so it was held tightly upwards against me. He picked up a piece of his shirt, put it under my nose...I could smell his scent on it—the strong cologne that he preferred. He moved the material down over my hard cock that was suspended upwards, and laid the cotton over it, lightly grinding his palm over it. I remember his lips were close to mine, but not much else; I was too hot.

When I regained my senses, I knew my load had already exploded, in my palm, upwards against my chest, everywhere.

He fell back into the chair, throwing one leg over the arm, studying my body, slowly stroking, I moved in close to him, leaning down and completing the job for him, one hand tightly under his balls, rubbing, the other cranking his cock until he gasp loudly and spewed straight up to his neck.

Exhausted, we took stock of each other, the shredded fabric everywhere and we both laughed.

Jake took the shreds of his shirt and wiped the sticky mess off his chest.

I used the scraps of his boxers to do the same thing on my own body.

"That was a blast," he commented."

"Yep." I got up and went upstairs to retrieve some clothes for us. When I returned, in faded *Wranglers* and an *Old Navy* t-shirt, with some gray sweat pants and a black tee for Jake, he was already on the phone, looking better than ever.

Too Good A Chance To Miss

Dan looked totally hot, as usual, as he stepped through the kitchen door. He was wearing a pair of faded and ripped *Nevada* jeans with a navy blue *Roots* sweatshirt and a blue denim jacket.

"Wow." Dan always looked pretty amazing; no matter what clothes he wore. The small rips in the thighs of his blue jeans showcased his legs nicely. One might almost think he had torn his jeans on purpose, just to show off his physique. I would not have put it past him, either.

I went out to light the barbeque, pulling on Dan's jacket just because it was closest to the patio door. The jacket was a little big on me, but not too badly oversized.

"So now you're wearing my clothes?" Dan asked as I stepped back inside.

"Yep. It's getting cold out there."

"You look good in denim," Fred told me. "He looks good in your clothes. You both look better naked."

"You're just saying that," Dan joked.

Fred shrugged and poured more of the cranberry-strawberry wine into our glasses.

"Maybe I should give you that jacket. It's getting a little snug for me to wear."

"You're putting on the pounds again."

"No, the material shrinks when I wash it."

"Sure it does, Dan." I headed back outside to put the steaks on the barbecue.

It was hard watching the movie after dinner. *Rocky Horror* always got me worked up.

Stealing glances at Dan didn't help matters either. His tight jeans accented his bulging crotch really nicely.

We were several drinks into the evening too, the three of us feeling nice and mellow. Inhibitions were wearing awfully thin.

I was thinking about making a move on him…just start rubbing his legs, maybe reach through the torn denim to stroke his warm bare flesh, and see what happened.

The phone rang.

Sighing, I stood up and headed to the kitchen and picked up the receiver after the fourth ring. "Hello."

"*Hello,*" Leanne's cheerful voice came back. "*We got home early.*"

Damn! "So how was the show?" I asked her sweetly.

"*It was good. How's my husband?*"

A loaded question indeed. "He's spectacular, as usual." I was walking back into the living room. "We have him tied up naked in our bedroom and Fred is having his way with him even as we speak."

Dan looked startled.

Fred just laughed.

"*Well tell him to get his clothes back on. I'm coming over.*"

"Kay. See ya shortly." I clicked the phone off. "Put your clothes back on guys. She's coming over."

Fred sighed. I knew that he had been hoping for more than just dinner and a movie with Dan. Our *guys' nights* usually got hot and steamy.

Leanne and Sue came in about ten minutes later. They told us all about murder mystery dinner they'd attended, then we returned to the living room to watch *Creature From The Black Lagoon*. I didn't see anything special about the two leads, but Fred and Sue and Leanne all enjoyed the spectacle of half-naked men walking around.

"I can't keep awake," Dan complained. "It's the medication I'm on."

Or the half bottle of rum he'd polished off, I thought. *All that liquor wasted!* We had done our best to get him half-corked so that we could jump him…and now his wife was there! *Damn it all!*

Dan staggered upstairs.

Fred and I stayed to watch the movie with the girls.

The movie didn't interest me too much and I half-heartedly skimmed a book. I thought about going off to bed, but that would be rude to our guests. "I need to use the facilities." I headed upstairs.

The movie was loud and I bypassed the bathroom. Dan was sprawled out, flat on his back on the spare bed. He was snoring.

I watched him for a moment, and then I stepped through the door.

I leaned over him to inhale the scent of his cologne. I gave him a gentle kiss, but he didn't respond.

My hand dropped down to the fly of his jeans.

His bulge was prominent.

Temptation…oh, the temptation!

The stairs in our house creaked so I knew I would have some warning if anyone else decided to head upstairs.

Why not?

With that, I unzipped him and reached inside his briefs.

His cock was soft and flaccid. I pulled it out to look at it. He was like me: a shower, not a grower. Then I licked it. I took it into my mouth, teasing the tip with my tongue.

Dan was getting hard…and he was still snoring.

I proceeded to take him all into my mouth, or at least as much as I could manage. Dan moaned softly, but he was sleeping as only a passed-out drunk can. He was really hard and really erect and I was enjoying myself immensely. The risk of knowing his wife was downstairs only made my heart beat faster.

I sucked him off, teasing him with my tongue. He moaned and shifted his legs slightly, and I thought he was awake, but he was still snoring. Still sleeping so peacefully. I kept sucking him until finally he shot, moaning softly in his sleep. I swallowed his entire load. Slightly salty, but still good.

I licked my lips. "Very nice, Dan." I slid his dick back into his pants and then zipped his fly back up with a smile on my own lips. "Very nice indeed."

I snagged a book from the bookcase in the master bedroom and went back downstairs.

"What took you so long?" Leanne asked.

"I was looking for a story I wanted to reread," I replied. "Couldn't find the book at first."

"Oh."

Fred never noticed a thing.

Starting Something

Fred headed upstairs to use the bathroom.

Dan climbed out of the glider and hurried over to the couch. "Quick, sit up!" he ordered.

I tossed my book onto the coffee table and sat up.

Dan plopped down and smiled at me.

Well, I had been wondering if he was going to start anything tonight or not. Looks like the answer was YES!

He reached over and rubbed his hand across the front of my black nylon pants. "You interested?" he asked.

"Always," I replied.

"Thought so." Dan unzipped the fly of his jeans and pushed them and his briefs down. His cock, at the moment, was relatively small and flaccid. He began to stroke it.

I pushed my pants and boxers down so that my own semi-hard cock could be seen. I also pushed my tee-shirt away from it, baring my chest. "Let me do that." I reached over and took hold of Dan's cock. "Oh yes, this does feel nice." He was rapidly getting hard.

I took my glasses off and set them on the table. I leaned in close and nuzzled Dan's cheek. "I like the new beard," I told him.

"I'm still not sure about it. I might let it grow in or I might just shave it all off." He kissed me and our tongues probed each other's mouths. I just totally loved the feel of his beard against my chin.

"Where is he?"

"Who cares?" I countered. "Or are you tired of me?" It was no secret that he thought Fred was hotter than me...which did Fred's ego some good and was a fact I could live with. I think Fred's hot after all.

Fred finally came back downstairs, apologizing for taking so long. He spotted us on the couch and froze in mid-word, as well as mid-step. He stared at the pair of us. "I see."

"You were saying?" I asked him. I was still stroking Dan and he was still stroking me and it felt wonderful.

"Coming over to join us?" Dan asked. "Or just cumming?"

Fred came towards the couch. Dan and I both reached for his jeans and began to rub the front. He was getting hard behind the fly.

"Let's head upstairs where there's more room." I never really enjoyed having sex on the couch. I much preferred to be in the bedroom.

We stood up and I pulled my pants up.

Fred practically ran up the stairs.

I grabbed Dan's ass. His jeans were still hanging open and his erection was bobbing. I grabbed it and squeezed. "Very, very nice, Dan."

He kissed me and my tongue probed the back of his throat.

We headed upstairs and I followed Dan's tight ass into the dimly lit bedroom. Fred was already lying naked on the bed. He had a nice erection of his own in his hand.

Shirtless, Dan shucked off his tight blue jeans. His briefs were tight against his body.

"Dan has such great taste in underwear," I commented.

"I prefer briefs to boxers," he replied. "I find boxers and boxer briefs chafe."

"I prefer boxers usually." I dropped my splash pants and briefs at the same time. "I prefer nothing at all even more." Naked, I walked over to Dan and kissed him. "Very nice.

I dropped to my knees and began to tease the tip of his cock with my tongue. He gasped and a shiver wracked his body.

I pulled Dan down onto the bed. I was lying on my back, with Dan on top of me. He rubbed his hard erection against mine—Fred often did something similar—and it felt really really good. Dan and I kissed each other deeply and passionately, our lips locked and our tongues probing deeply into each other's mouths.

I was stroking Fred's cock with one hand and Dan's with another. Someone's hand was stroking mine—no idea who it belonged too and at that moment, I didn't care. Fred and Dan were kissing and it was hot watching them go at it.

I struggled to reach Fred's cock with my mouth.

"Don't worry about me."

"Nonsense, we want you to cum first."

Dan shifted position slightly and Fred's cock slipped into my mouth. I sucked at it, licking the tip with my tongue and teasing him. He squirmed in what I hoped was genuine pleasure.

Fred moaned. I reached for his nipples and began to stroke them.

Still kneeling, Fred moaned and shot his load across my chest.

I scooped up gooey cum and rubbed against Dan's cock. "Oh yeah, feel how hard you are."

"Faster!" Dan winced. "Faster, Mike, please. I'm getting so close."

"Good." Fred kissed him hard.

I rubbed faster.

Dan grunted. "Oh god!" His thick cum splashed across my stomach.

"Oh yeah!" I caught most of the cum in my hands and used it as lube for myself. I felt two tongues working my nipples and I groaned. "Oh yeah!" I shot so forcefully that cum splashed my neck.

"Wow, you spurted." Fred shook his head in wonder. "You hardly ever shoot like that."

I just gurgled something weakly in reply.

Dinner Guest

I was passing through the mall doors when I spotted a really hot blond. He was walking towards me with his hands full of packages and bags.

I held the door open for him. He smiled and offered me a quick "Thanks". His voice was smooth and his words came easily, without shyness.

He was in his twenties, close to five foot nine, with blonde hair and a dark mustache. The mustache actually looked great on his face, unlike that of most men I know. I hadn't looked close enough yet to pay attention to his eye color, but the eyes were warm and friendly. He looked at me as we stood there a moment longer, then he offered me a shy smile, and I smiled back. I just managed to say "See ya" as I finished going inside the

He nodded. "Take it easy"

As the doors closed behind me, I rolled my eyes and let all sorts of wonderful fantasies flow through my head. I wanted to know more about him. Probably wasn't going to happen though...just a chance passing that would never amount to anything else.

A few steps later it struck me! That was Hotty Scotty!

I whirled around and headed back towards the doors. I scanned the parking lot with desperate eyes, but there was no sign of him. "Damn!"

Funnily enough, I saw him just a couple of hours later.

I was in the supermarket on a Saturday late afternoon cruising up and down the aisles looking for some dinner ideas. I came into the cereal aisle and there was Scotty.

"Hi." He spoke first. I loved the sound of his voice.

"Hi. What's for dinner?" I asked him jokingly.

He snickered. "Haven't decided yet. How about you?"

"Chicken Parmesan, I think, though cooking it isn't always the easiest."

"Yeah, I hear that. I've gotten used to cooking for just one, but that doesn't mean I always like it." His voice was drawing me in. It was just so confident and easy. "So how's Fred doing?"

My jaw dropped. "That's why you look familiar!" Hotty Scotty! "Your face has been playing around my mind all day but I couldn't place it." I decided to lie to him...let's not mention our first and only encounter. Unless he wanted to mention it first that is.

"It took me a while to recall your name too, Mike." He offered me another of his shy smiles. "Damn, it's good to see you again."

"It's been years." I shook my head.

"Yeah."

"You live nearby? How about coming for dinner? Chicken parm is my best dish." I was being forward, unlike my usual style, but Scotty was really hot and it had been a long time since Fred and I had seen him around. He kinda dropped out of touch with us after that night in the apartment.

We continued to walk together through the aisles. "Sounds nice."

"We have a house now." I gave him the address.

"Cool. I was thinking about stopping by the apartment sometime to see how you guys were doing."

"So come to the house now. I can have dinner ready for 7:30, but why not come over sooner. I could use a hand if you don't mind. Can you come over at say sixish?"

"Sure. Looking forward to it."

I gave him my address again. "Same phone number." We talked as we finished grocery shopping. I left to finish other errands as well.

A few minutes before six, the doorbell rang. Scotty was dressed in khakis, boots, and a denim shirt, a nice change from the blue jeans, polo shirt, and sneakers from earlier today. He looked and smelled nice, apparently having showered as well. I too had showered and changed into corduroy slacks and a button-down shirt. Fred was in black jeans and a blue-white checked shirt. I asked what he liked for music and turned on the stereo, then got us some coolers from the fridge.

We sat together outside on the deck, enjoying the warm sun and clear
air. For about a half-hour we got reacquainted, listened to the music, and
got comfortable with each other. I felt my crotch stirring, as it usually did, as we talked. Scotty was evidently having the same feelings and adjusted his crotch twice. He apologized when I looked at him as he was making the
adjustment the second time.

"No sweat. To tell you the truth, you uh..."

"Turn you on?"

"Yeah." He blushed. He looked like such a hot, confident stud and yet he was really just so shy! "I've been thinking about that last night...."

I reached over and took his hand. Fred put his hand on Scotty's leg. We sat and looked at each other for a few minutes.

"Come on," Fred said.

We all stood up and went inside. We reached the living room and sat down on the sofa. He looked me square in the eyes and kissed me. By the way, his eyes are green. One hand held my hand and the other went around
my shoulder. I too embraced him as we kissed, feeling the warmth and the
moisture of his lips, and exploring his mouth with my tongue. His breath
tasted like mint. His handsome face smiled as we kissed. I couldn't help but smile back, and kissed him over and over.

"You're really hot," he told me as we kissed.

Well, I don't know that I'd use the term hot to describe myself, but I can hold my own in a crowd of good-looking men. "Hey, just look who's talking about hot," I said as I looked at him. "You are gorgeous, buddy. You must be beating the girls off with a stick."

He laughed. "Yeah, sometimes."

We sat back, held hands, kicked off our shoes, put our feet up on the

coffee table, and wrapped one arm around each other. We kissed again, talked some more, and forgot all about dinner. He stood up, took me by the hand, and led me to the middle of the floor where we began to slow dance to the music. I put both my arms around Scotty, looked into his eyes, and kissed him as we danced. His arms held me close.

Fred just sat there, watching us with a smile on his face. He looked like he was enjoying the sight of us kissing so I kissed Scotty all the harder.

We ignored the few commercials and continued to hold each other and dance. He told me of his fantasies about me and I returned my fantasies about him. "You've got a hard-on," he said as I let his hand slide across it.

He turned me around, held me from behind, and slid his hand over my slacks, feeling me, making me harder. He kissed my neck. "You taste so good, bud."

"You both look really hot," Fred told us. "And I can't wait any longer. Let's get upstairs." The front of his jeans were unzipped and his cock was erect.

I took his hand again and led him upstairs into the bedroom.

"Lay down, let me undress you," I said.

He did.

I took off his socks, straddled him and unbuttoned his shirt as I kissed him on his lips, chin, neck, sucked his Adam's apple, and worked down to his chest as I exposed it little by little. He still had that Superman tattoo on his arm. I unbuckled his slacks and slowly unzipped them. He had no briefs on underneath and I saw the tip of his uncut cock and then the length of the hard organ as I exposed it and slid his slacks off.

I touched it and stroked it to full hardness. His face told me that he loved the feel of my hands gently stroking him. I lay between his legs and began to lick his cock, slowly moving up and down, from the tip to his balls. I sucked each of his balls, and then both, into my mouth. I licked back up to the tip of his cock, opened my mouth, and slid his cock inside. He let his head drop back as he leaned on his elbows and moaned. The seven-inch length was smooth and tasted as sweet as any cock I've ever had. He closed his eyes and rested against the pillows while I gave him my best effort at pleasing him.

Fred leaned in close and was kissing him. They were both trading some serious tongue-action.

I let Scotty's cock slip from my mouth, took off my shirt, slacks, and socks and laid beside him, naked, the heat of our bodies melting together. His scent smelled of fresh soap and light cologne. He reached for my dick as I held his. We fondled each other, kissed, and then moved into the sixty-nine

position so that we could both suck each other.

His tongue and lips worked up and down the full length of my throbbing flesh. He licked at the purple knob. Then he opened his lips and went down the entire length of my rigid cock, sliding it in and out of his mouth several times before continuing to lick it from head to balls. He was gentle and talented, eating my dick like he'd done it every day.

Had he? I wondered. It had been years since that night back at the apartment. He was not this gentle back then. A nice change from the rough and clumsiness I remembered. I did to him what he did to me. We were taking good care of each other, enjoying sucking each other's cock as much as we enjoyed being sucked. Scotty was all that

that was all that mattered to me, and his pleasure was all that I wanted to fulfill. He was handsome, quiet, mild mannered, and considerate. He obviously enjoyed sucking cock and pleasing his partner. I wonder if he'd had many.

"No, not many really," he murmured, as if reading my mind. "But I sure do enjoy a man's cock in my mouth. Let's take a break and talk some more."

Fred and I leaned in close, holding him so we could talk about his past a bit. We let our hands idly roam across each other's bodies.

He started. "I had a buddy in high school that I used to fool around with. Mostly it was getting together to jack off whenever we could. Then one afternoon after school, he taught me about sucking. I've had a hunger for cock ever since. I've had one long relationship in recent years but he's moved out of the province. When I spotted you in the store and realized you were you, I was really hoping you'd be what I was looking for. By the way, you are."

I laughed.

Fred gave him a quick kiss on the cheek. "You were great that night, Scotty. Mike and I have talked about you several times since them."

"We wondered what you had gotten up too. You just kinda vanished from our lives."

Scotty blushed. He still had a really boyish smile on his face.

"We thought we might have scared you off or something."

"No way, guys. I just got busy."

"You're not busy now?"

"No."

I glanced down at his slender, smooth body and smiled as his uncut cock twitched. "Reminds me of college. I went out drinking with this one buddy of mine and we ended up back at his place after a few drinks. Talk led to groping and that led to us getting naked. I was curious and he knew it."

"He was gay?"

"Oh yeah." I nodded. "The first taste of cock I ever had made me know that cock was what I wanted. I even got to fuck him a couple of times, but we loved sucking each other."

"What happened to him?"

"Different classes and different schedules. We lost touch."

"Lucky for me," Fred commented.

We there lay silently for a while.

"I just want to hold you, bud. No need to worry about pleasing me. You already have. I'm glad I met up with you in the store today."

"Yeah," I admitted, "me too. My heart skipped a couple of beats when I saw you. I was really happy to see you in the grocery store."

"I was surprised when Mike told me you were coming by." Fred smiled at him. "Really happy."

After a while, I moved down between his legs, moved his legs up on to my back, and resumed sucking his now flaccid cock. In no time he was rock hard again, moaning, and letting me service him. He smiled down at me when I looked up into his eyes. He dropped his head backward again, and let a moan escape his throat. In a few more minutes of sucking his stiff, fleshy cock, I tasted pre-cum on the head of his cock.

Fred was kissing him again.

I increased the action on his cock a little, keeping the cock firmly in my mouth. He began to cum so I sucked him deeper into my mouth. I jacked him until his balls were drained of their sweet milky white load, until my mouth was wet with a fresh load of cream.

"How was that?" I asked, really wanting to know.

He didn't answer, except for putting me on my back and laying between my muscular legs, eating my cock for all he was worth, sucking up and down, gently, carefully, hungrily, and with a talent equal to few other guys I had met. When he tasted of my pre-cum, he knew I was close. He kept up his steady pace, enjoying the taste of my meat as much as the expectation of a reward. My breathing changed and he was soon jacking a load of spunk equal in volume to his own. He swallowed, some of it dripping out of the corner of his mouth. He licked it up with his tongue.

When I was jacked dry, he lay on top of me and kissed me. He smiled and I returned the smile with great sincerity. His handsome face did not show ego or unkindness.

We talked some more as we lay together. Once again he reached for my cock, fondling it to erection.

"What, you're ready for more?" I asked as he licked up and down my shaft and then sucked it into his moist mouth.

"Yeah, except this time I want to feel you inside me. Do you have any lube?"

I got out of bed and went to the nightstand. When I returned, he took the lube from me and then rubbed it onto my cock. Once I was nice and hard, he spread his legs for me. First, I knelt down, lifted his legs and rimmed his ass, tasting the hot sweet wetness of his puckered hole. My tongue found his sweet spot and licked for several minutes. I stood, moved his ass to the edge of my bed, and put his legs over my shoulders. I put a little more lube on my cock, and then entered him in one smooth motion.

Once inside him, I left my cock right where it was, deep up inside his ass, to let him get used to it. His asshole was incredibly tight and inviting, and he clenched my cock with his ring of muscle. I slowly withdrew, up to the head, and then slid it back in his ass. I did this a few times to get a rhythm going. He moaned softly as I fucked him, slowly sliding in and out of his tight eager asshole. He clenched and unclenched with the rhythm of a master, making my cock feel the tightness and wetness of his insides. I changed our position slightly, enough that I could lean forward and kiss him while I fucked his ass.

He smiled, moaned, closed his eyes, and told me to fuck him good.

I did.

For twenty minutes, he and I worked with each other to bring about the most glorious orgasm that I've experienced in six years. I shot deeply inside his hot, wet asshole. His ass sucked my cum, draining me thoroughly. Once spent, I leaned forward and licked it slowly off his skin. He pulled me down on top of him and kissed me warmly, thanking me for the intense good pleasure I gave to his ass.

I looked deep in his eyes. He was just too pretty for his own good.

"Can I fuck you?" he asked sincerely. "I don't know if you are actually into that, but..."

"There's no way I'd refuse you, man. It's been a while, but I'd love you to fuck me, just like I did to you."

And fuck me he did. Except fuck seems too harsh a word for his ability to fill me with his man muscle. He made sweet love to my ass, much in the way I did to his, only better. His strokes were slow and deep, no pain to be found, even in the initial assault of entry. He knew how to use his cock to

please a man. He kissed me as he slid inside me, filling me with his sweet breath and his hard cock at the same time.

Fred was playing with my nipples and I gripped his cock with my hands, stroking him into ecstasy.

For nearly twenty minutes, I was the focus of their love making, of their heat, of their kindness. Scotty pulled out of my ass, straddled my torso, and let me jack the cream from his hard dick, into my mouth. He ate some of his load from the edge of my chin.

Fred moaned as he came and his cum splattered across Scotty's chest and mine as well.

We collapsed into a sweaty heap.

Scotty closed his eyes and sighed.

Fred fell on top of me, smiled brightly, and kissed me again, letting his tongue explore the recesses of my mouth. I held on to him, feeling fulfilled like never before, knowing he was equally content. I didn't have to guess; it was in his eyes.

We finally made a light dinner and returned to the bed a few hours later,

where we slept peacefully. We made love again on Sunday morning, in no

hurry to get out of bed. Scotty was a good man and a new friend. We were all looking forward to keeping our newly rediscovered friendship intact. I, for one, was looking forward to many good times, in and out of bed, with him.

"Yeah, me too," he said when I made that comment.

Also by Frank Sol

Novels Of The Sensual City
A Family Affair
Delivering The Goods
Divine Punishment
Good Neighbours
Just Between Friends

Novels On The Prairies
Bareback Range
Return To Bareback Range
Fenced In